# DEATH OF A NOBODY

Charlie Pegg has an obscure and dangerous source of income. He works as a police informer – a precarious and dangerous operation. But Charlie is also a skilled joiner and when he starts to work at Old Mead Park, a luxury block of flats, he quickly sees opportunities for combining both lines of work.

Superintendent Lambert has found Charlie a reliable source of information over the years, so when he offers to deliver drug dealer and gangland boss James Berridge into the policeman's hands, Lambert is eager to buy what Charlie has to sell . . . After all, Berridge has proved an elusive villain, but the greater the prize, the greater the danger, as Charlie is to discover. . .

Lambert and Hook, those most human of detectives, bring flair and experience to their latest investigation, and J. M. Gregson displays his customary sense of place and talent for realistic dialogue, making this Lambert and Hook mystery his most gripping yet.

BY THE SAME AUTHOR

WATERMARKED
STRANGLEHOLD
THE FOX IN THE FOREST
DEAD ON COURSE
BRING FORTH YOUR DEAD
FOR SALE – WITH CORPSE
MURDER AT THE NINETEENTH

# DEATH OF A
# NOBODY

## J. M. Gregson

HarperCollins*Publishers*

Collins Crime
An imprint of HarperCollins*Publishers*
77–85 Fulham Palace Road, London W6 8JB

First published in Great Britain
in 1995 by Collins Crime

1 3 5 7 9 10 8 6 4 2

© J. M. Gregson 1995

The Author asserts the moral right to be
identified as the author of this work

A catalogue record for this book is
available from the British Library

ISBN 0 00 232554 3

Set in Meridien and Bodoni

Photoset by Rowland Phototypesetting Ltd
Bury St Edmunds, Suffolk
Printed and bound in Great Britain by
HarperCollinsManufacturing Glasgow

# 1

An evening in early April. Warm for the time of the year, but with the prospect of a rapid drop in temperature and a still night. All around the sense of nature erupting into growth: spring is pushing forward insistently in the west of England.

Nowhere is more green, and it is a green full of the promises of things to come. In this part of Gloucestershire, the country life still runs strongly, and the weekenders have not taken over the village housing, as they have in the fashionable sectors of the Cotswolds which lie to the north. The smoke rises in slender grey columns from the cottage chimneys as the chill descends with the dew upon the fields. The predominant sound is that of the new lambs searching out their mothers and being answered by the ewes.

The field patterns have not altered as much here as they have on the factory farms further south. For a little while, those with the fancy to do so might imagine themselves transported back in time for a century and more. The illusion would disappear, of course, with the first human presence and the first human activity.

For the greenery in the middle distance is neither pasture nor meadow. The wide avenue of closely mown grass between the rows of trees, the telltale smear of sand at the distant end of the vista, reveal that this is in fact a golf course. There are few people upon it as the early spring darkness approaches. But the solitary figure who eventually appears removes any delusions that this scene is anything but a contemporary one.

He is a tall man, so that he makes good pace, even when

he seems to be taking a leisurely course towards the tiny white speck around which his activity revolves. He weaves a rather zigzag track along the green valley between the stands of trees, pausing reflectively beside his trolley for an instant of evaluation after each stroke.

This solitary golfer is upright and grey-haired, well over six feet tall, so that when he settles over the ball to play, he has to stoop a little, making the clubs seem a fraction too short for him. He manifests no outward discontent after an indifferent shot, for time has taught him to be philosophical about his performance. He is over fifty, his shoulders already rounded a little towards the stoop which comes to tall men with age, though he seems lean and well-preserved.

He is that quintessential representative of late twentieth-century working life, a Superintendent of Police.

Superintendent John Lambert was enjoying himself. Although not all of his drives had been perfect, he had not missed a fairway from the tee. And he had hit two good four-irons, watching with satisfaction as the ball flew high and long against the darkening blue of the spring evening.

Above all, he appeared to have the course to himself. The clocks had been put forward scarcely more than a week before, and not many people had yet attuned themselves to the fact that it was possible to play a few holes in the evening. He enjoyed this solitary progress, feeling mind and body unwind after a day spent in the frustrations of bureaucracy.

There were not many better places in the world to be on an evening like this. It was the kind of weather people went to Portugal to enjoy, though they were not always successful in the quest. He would irritate Christine by parading that thought before her once again, when he got home for his belated supper. He hit a long drive from the sixth tee; only at the top of its flight did it move lazily to the right, as the slice he had never quite mastered asserted itself again. But the ball was still on the fairway, and as he moved towards it over the rise of the ground, he caught the last of the sun on the western slopes of the nearby Malverns.

He did not know that he was being watched.

He looked at the lush new green of the fields between him and the Malverns and thought of the father who was dead and of the lines he loved to quote:

> *Now fades the glimmering landscape on the sight,*
> *And all the air a solemn stillness holds,*
> *Save where the beetle wheels his droning flight,*
> *And drowsy tinklings lull the distant folds.*

Well, it was not yet summer. And if it was as still on the next hole as on this one, he would hear not the beetle but the distant hum of the traffic on the M50. But he wished, with a tender, welcome pain, that the old man was still at his elbow, to approve his progress and quote 'Gray's Elegy' at him whenever the opportunity arose.

The man who watched him across the width of two fairways knew none of this affectionate melancholy. Within the three-sided shed whose floor was scored by the studs of a thousand sheltering golfers, he waited patiently for his man. He had noted with satisfaction that he was alone.

Lambert saw the first evening star and knew that the light would not endure much longer. He used the star as his line on the par three: it shone just to the left of the motionless flag, above the oak tree whose skeleton was still bare as the sap rose within it. If he could hit a gentle six-iron and allow his fade to bring the ball in towards the hole . . .

There was the harsh ugly sound of a thinned shot. The ball flew at half the height it should have done, curving fast into the deep bunker to the right of the green, burying itself resentfully in the steep wall of sand. 'You stupid bugger!' he muttered to himself. There was feeling but little anger in the words; he had played enough to expect at least one of these in a round. Playing alone, he could persuade himself that it was merely a lapse of concentration, rather than a flaw of technique.

He got the ball on to the edge of the green with his sand wedge, but did not bother to putt. He shivered for the first time as he hurried to the next tee. The temperature was falling quickly now: there would be a frost tonight. This hole would have to be his last.

He was almost at the green when he saw the man signalling from the shelter. He recognized him immediately, for they had met here before. It was a rendezvous more safe from prying eyes than the obscurest city warehouse. That was important to both of them, but particularly to the man who came towards him now without a word of greeting. Secrecy was more than important to him: it might represent the difference between life and death.

Once he was sure that Lambert had seen him, he slipped back into the shelter of the battered hut like a guilty thing. His shiftiness was habitual, but on this occasion it was justified. Had he been seen in conversation with a senior policeman, he would have been in extreme danger.

Lambert gave no sign that he had noticed this presence, playing his own small part in the little charade of deception for the watchers that could surely not be present in this quiet place. He went towards the unseen visitor with a mixture of revulsion and excitement.

Revulsion because this man was a snout; a grass; an informer; whatever was the latest word which the criminal faction and the police who fought it agreed upon. No one likes a grass, even when he is bringing valuable information to the fight against crime. He is the worst sort of mercenary, the one who sells his treachery for money.

But the superintendent felt excitement as well as he trudged with studious deliberation towards the peeling blue paint of the hut. He was an old-fashioned thief-taker, in an era when superintendents were increasingly regarded as senior, desk-bound management. He was a hunter, and the adrenaline rose at the prospect of information which might take him nearer to a quarry.

Charlie Pegg would not have risked his neck by coming here unless he had something to offer. There was an understanding between the two men which had been built over years of discreet exchange. A jaded perception of their worth to each other had grown now into a grudging respect.

Lambert bent to the wheel of his trolley, pretending to

make a small adjustment, feeling ridiculous as he was drawn into the snout's world of sly contrivance. He found himself speaking from the side of his mouth as he said, 'Well, Charlie? You've got something for me?'

There was no reply until he had eased himself into the open-sided shed and perched himself on the single bench which was all the shelter afforded. He squeezed his right side against the boards of the hut's side, automatically avoiding any physical contact with the man beside him. It was as though the man was a carrier for the disease of betrayal, so that even to touch him might bring the risk of defilement.

'It's worth money, this, Mr Lambert. Big money.' The wheedling tone made the claim an appeal, not a statement. A man like this might bring much gold to a detective, but he had the mien as well as the appearance of a mendicant, not a salesman.

'We'll decide how much it's worth in due course, Charlie. You know how it works – you should do by now.'

The man beside him nodded. Even that small gesture was furtive, as if it might somehow betray him in the semi-darkness of the hut; his eyes darted from side to side before he spoke again. 'You've looked after me well enough in the past, Mr Lambert. I trust you, you know.'

In the other, larger section of his life, Charlie Pegg was an excellent craftsman, reliable in his work. His customers found him a likeable man; to at least two people, he was even lovable. But in the role he had here, he was like an ill-treated dog, fawning hopefully at the feet of a stranger.

Lambert wanted suddenly to be rid of him. There seemed no escape from his bad breath in the narrow confines of this strange meeting place. He said, 'The sooner this is over the better, for both of us.' He peered round the edge of the shed, as if he expected men were going to appear from the gathering darkness; perhaps he was catching Pegg's mannerisms.

It was enough to hasten on his informant. 'I'm going to get Berridge for you, Mr Lambert. Something big, this time.'

'How big?' Lambert studied the scratch on the toe of his left golf shoe, as if it were of more interest to him than what was coming next. He concealed his excitement at the mention of that name. No one afforded a snout a high sense of his value; that was one of the first CID precepts he had learned, twenty years and more ago.

'Very big. The biggest.'

'We need evidence, Charlie. You know that. Witnesses, probably. That's what you need to deliver, to get much of a price.'

'I'll give you evidence. And some other names. Perhaps next time. There's going to be a big deal made, you see.'

Lambert pursed his lips, pretending to give consideration to whether he intended to go ahead with this at all. But he knew he did: the name had been enough to ensure that.

'Berridge, you say. Dangerous man for you to tangle with, Charlie. We want him, I won't deny it. And you say that you can deliver him to us. But what crime, Charlie? We want him put away for a long time.'

'Me too, Mr Lambert.' Pegg leaned forward, turning to look up more directly into the superintendent's face. He dropped his voice. 'I need him away for a long time, too, don't I?'

'You will if he finds out you were involved.' Lambert smiled grimly, turning the screw a little, trying to ensure that this pathetic specimen spilled everything in his desperate desire to protect his skin.

Pegg nodded vigorously. He looked outside automatically to ensure that the fairway was indeed deserted, unconsciously savouring this rare moment of melodrama in his uneventful life. He had to moisten his lips to deliver the important phrase.

'You'll get him this time, Mr Lambert. It's murder, you see.'

# 2

The big BMW stayed in the fast lane for over a mile; at this time of night, the motorway was quiet, especially the westbound carriageway which carried the traffic away from London.

He was fifty miles from the capital now, watching the needle creep towards the hundred, then reluctantly easing his foot off the pedal of the big automatic to control his speed. You couldn't just rely on your rear-view mirror, nowadays. There were all kinds of speed traps, each one more sophisticated than the last. Pity the pigs hadn't something more important to occupy their expensive resources – he allowed the motorist's automatic moan to creep into his mind. Then he smiled: it was a good thing for him and his enterprises that the police frittered away their resources on such harmless pursuits.

All the same, he dropped his speed to eighty as he went past the Swindon turning; he had no desire to raise his profile with the police, even if it was for no more than a speeding offence. The temperature had dropped sharply outside, but it was warm and comfortable as always in the BMW. He had restricted himself as usual to two gins and tonics in his office at the gaming club in London, but he must guard against the drowsiness that came with comfort and a steady cruising speed on a quiet motorway. He was reaching for the radio switch when the car phone bleeped.

He had thought it might be the Soho club he had left an hour earlier. But it was Murray, his manager at the Curvy Cats in Bristol. He was nervous at the start, as always; he sounded like a bank clerk, not a man who hired and fired

11

the musclemen which every strip club had to have around. 'I thought I'd better just keep you in the picture, sir. In case you didn't manage to get in here this week . . .' He left the words hanging in the air, hoping for the assurance of information about the owner's plans. Murray didn't like car phones, because you never knew whether the man on the other end of the line was hundreds of miles away or just round the corner.

The man in the speeding car knew that, too. He smiled a little in the darkness and withheld the information his caller wanted. 'Thank you, Murray. And the picture is?'

'The man they attended to is in hospital. Bristol General. He has a broken arm and three broken ribs. The sister says he'll probably be discharged tomorrow.' He poured out the facts hurriedly, like a child who knows the game is up and wants to get all the worst facts of his confession out in one breath.

The voice from the car phone did not change; it would have been impossible to deduce from its tone whether this news was welcome or otherwise. But in Bristol, Murray knew this was a black mark against his sector of the business. 'Was it near the club?'

'No. Three miles or more away. Outside the man's hotel.'

'Will he bring charges?'

'I don't think so. I don't see how he can. There's nothing to connect it with us. And Briggs says he wasn't recognized.' Murray was too eager again, now that he had reached the mitigating features. He had planned to get them in first; now he was anxious that if he did not speak quickly the boss would ring off and he would not be able to record them at all.

'What were your orders to him?'

'To frighten him off, that was all. Minimal force, if it was necessary at all. They should never have done that much damage. Briggs enjoys working people over too much, that's the trouble.'

'So why did you hire him?'

He had walked into that. The sudden volley of crackles as the car phone passed under overhead cables sounded like a

12

mocking chorus to Murray, as he struggled to formulate his answer. 'I – I thought I could control him. And on the occasions when we need real violence, he's one of the best. Swift and hard, and –'

'Get rid of him.'

'Oh. Are you sure, sir? I could give him a bollocking and tell him to make sure –'

'Send him on his way, Murray. And make sure that his sidekick knows that your orders are to be obeyed to the letter next time.'

'Right, sir. And I'll –'

'And make sure it doesn't happen again, eh, Murray?'

The line went dead before Murray could lurch into his assurances.

The man in the car smiled at his little demonstration of power. Keep the troops up to the mark, and you solved most of the problems at the outset. Then you could concern yourself with policy, not the day-to-day skirmishing. He had never been much good at violence himself. Now, when it was merely a case of deploying others to do his bidding, he found it easy to be both ruthless and clear-sighted.

He had been toying with the idea of going into the club at Bristol to see Murray. Now he decided that his authority had been effectively asserted through the more impersonal medium of his car phone. So he stayed on the M4 and paid the toll to swing between the high towers of the Severn Bridge. The tide was in and he caught the twinkle of lights on the estuary far below him. For a moment, he wondered about all those different lives in that watery world of which he was so totally ignorant.

Then he swung the car on to the A48, catching a glimpse of the massive walls of Chepstow Castle against the clear night sky as he skirted the town and moved to the north. Soon he would be in Oldford. The small market town was a suitably sleepy hideaway for a man who operated the businesses that brought in his money. And it was, after all, where his roots lay. There had been Berridges here for over two centuries, since his ancestors had moved in to work in the small mines of the Forest of Dean. Respectable men, who had accumulated a little capital and moved up in the world. Now the latest Berridge was putting those inherited resources to darker, much more lucrative uses.

It was nearly midnight now, and the main shopping street was deserted as the light-blue BMW moved almost silently along it. He had time to glance up at the old-fashioned façade with its suits and sweaters behind the plate-glass windows and the elaborate raised gold letters over the top that spelled out 'Jas Berridge and Sons'.

There was another, slightly bigger version of this shop in Gloucester. His grandfather had bought the premises in the dark days of 1930, and his father had built the business to a modest prosperity in the palmy days after Hitler's war. For the latest James Berridge in his BMW, the shops were no more than a respectable frontage for the more dubious dealings and establishments where he made his real money. Money his ancestors would never have dreamed of. From activities which would have appalled them.

He had managers in these two shops, and he scarcely ever interfered with them. When he made suggestions, they came with the half-apologetic air and the obsolete courtesy which the latest James Berridge thought might have come from his father or grandfather. He saw himself as a man of many roles, and this one amused him hugely, so that he gave full attention to the part and studied with interest the effects he was making as he delivered his lines. There was no doubt that he was successful in it. The local community thought of him as highly respectable. Those of them who paused to think were sometimes surprised that there was such money to be made from old-fashioned gents' outfitting in this competitive age; but someone would always offer the suggestion of 'private money', that mysterious and wholly satisfactory source of affluence that was otherwise without explanation.

Berridge's wife must have brought him money, they said. She had the cut-glass accent and the wardrobe to support that view. They were not to know that she was from an ancient but impecunious family, which had been quite relieved to consign her to the persistent and agreeably wealthy young man who had arrived among their set after

14

a short-service commission in the Royal Horse Artillery.

That had been twenty years and more ago, and Gabrielle, like her family, knew much more about James Berridge now. But at least the affluence they had anticipated had continued. Indeed, it had developed quite remarkably. Gabrielle, whatever her unhappiness, had never been short of money and the trappings it could bring.

The name 'Old Mead Park', picked out in raised gold lettering on the dark green board by the entrance, was merely the developer's acknowledgement of the fine old mansion he had demolished. The four-storey block of flats which had replaced it was the most luxurious new building in the Oldford area. And the spacious penthouse which occupied half of the top storey was the most opulent unit in the whole complex. It was important to its owner that it was conspicuously the best: it established the position Berridge wished to assert for himself in his local context, without bringing the attention which an older building like a stately home might have attracted.

He had other images in other places. The London flat by Regent's Park where he entertained a succession of mistresses was in a Nash terrace, more expensive but more discreet than this one. And the small house in the centre of Amsterdam was totally anonymous, purely a residence for the questionable business which he conducted from time to time within it.

The garage door beneath the flats rose quietly at the command of Berridge's electronic control. He rolled the BMW to a halt and did not trouble to set the alarm as the door shut behind him. There was no porter here at this hour, but the lift carried him silently up to the top storey. Gabrielle's room, as he had expected, was in darkness; he rarely told her nowadays when she might expect him home.

He went out through the patio doors to look for a moment at the night and the blue-black universe outside. Some day he might fulfil the fancy of many years and build himself an observatory. Not here; somewhere more private, with gardens and ancient trees around him. The dome and the telescope would need to be somewhere isolated. It would not be until he was finished with all this and retired, a respected figure, offering no threat to anyone. Some day . . .

He left the cool peace of the April night and went into his study. He put the documents he had brought from the car into the bottom drawer of the desk and relocked it carefully, as he always did. Something about the papers on the top of the desk struck him as he was about to move out. He turned them over cautiously. Nothing was missing. But they had been rearranged, as if someone had looked through them in search of interesting material, and put them back in a slightly different manner. Jim Berridge was a methodical man, and he was sure of it.

Not Gabrielle, he thought. She made a point of her contemptuous ignorance of his dealings; and she knew well enough that nothing of great interest would be left available to prying eyes. And not the cleaner: she had strict instructions that she was not even to set foot in this room, and she was too well paid to ignore them. Who, then?

Jim Berridge sat at his desk and gave careful consideration to the possibilities. Then he went to bed and was asleep within minutes.

# 3

Christine Lambert watched her husband surreptitiously at the breakfast table. He had protested about the muesli when she had switched him to it; now he ate it each morning with some relish. She had too much sense and experience to point that out to him, for she knew that he would merely reply dolefully that you could get used to anything, then embark on a eulogy for his departed eggs and bacon.

Usually he was out of the house before she left for her school. When he was not, she found herself running unexpectedly late. It was so this morning. She was studying the advance of grey hairs into his still plentiful crop as it bent over the newspaper when she realized the time; she flew to her Fiesta with her briefcase still unfastened and books threatening to spew from it. John came and opened the gates for her and waved her off, enjoying the moment of unaccustomed domesticity and the illusion that he was behaving like an orthodox young husband.

Then he went back into the trim bungalow, made a phone call to Rushton in the CID section, washed the few breakfast dishes, and read again the note by the phone in Christine's writing, recording that his daughter Caroline would be here at the weekend with her husband and the children. It would be good to see them, he told himself conventionally. It would also be a noisy and boisterous time in the normally quiet bungalow. Well, there was always the golf club — or he could take the golden retriever which would arrive with the rest of the family for a walk: he always liked doing that. He must be getting old.

He went into the garden, enjoying the bright, crisp

morning, inspecting the promising red shoots of foliage on the neatly pruned roses, assessing the chances that a late frost might set them back. Retired policemen traditionally grew roses. Well, he might as well get ready for it; retirement was something he'd have to contemplate, in a few years. He left it vaguely at that 'few years', though precision was one of the necessities of his working life.

Against his will, he fell again to wondering about Charlie Pegg. Perhaps he should have pushed him harder last night, but his instincts had told him the little snout would come up with something more tangible in a few days. He felt the old surge of impatience that he had known twenty years and more ago as a young detective constable when a case hung fire. He was counting no chickens, but it would raise the morale of the whole CID section if they could pin down Jim Berridge.

He sniffed the invigorating morning air like an animal in search of its prey. There was plenty of the hunter left beneath Superintendent Lambert's grey hairs.

Detective Inspector Christopher Rushton set about his task with relish. It would help to show the chief the value of modern technology.

Old John Lambert had his virtues, of course he had. He was a shrewd, intuitive detective, a thief-taker of the old school. More crucially for Chris Rushton, he was almost unique among modern superintendents in conducting his investigations in the field rather than from the incident room. That had allowed Rushton the opportunity to act as data coordinator in the solving of several serious crimes, and he was grateful for that. It was the man bringing things together in the incident room who drew the attention of the top brass most easily. But Lambert could be scathing about the computers which were so important in keeping up with the increasing subtlety of contemporary criminal techniques. This assignment would show him how useful electronic filing and searching could be in the hands of a skilled operator.

After two hours, the stream of Rushton's enthusiasm was running less strongly. Even in the violent nineties, the number of unsolved killings which were quietly pigeonholed (the official line was that the files were never closed) as police failures was not as large as the public chose to think. The national list was now readily available on Rushton's computer, but there were few of them with local connections, and none involving the particular people he was seeking to link up with them.

There was another, longer group of violent crimes, which had to be registered officially as unsolved, though that adjective riled the CID. These were the ones where there was reasonable certainty about the perpetrator, but insufficient evidence to bring a case to court. Sometimes the police themselves reluctantly acknowledged that fact – as they had been forced to do at least twice in the case of James Berridge. Sometimes there were bitter arguments between CID men who had worked long and hard to bring villains to justice and the Crown Prosecution Service, who claimed from their more objective viewpoint that what had been presented to them was not the material for a case they could expect to win.

Rushton flashed these infuriating files up successively on his screen. Some of the local ones he already knew, of course, but he went further afield, looking painstakingly for connections between any violent deaths in the south of England and the men who interested him on the patch of Oldford CID. Any policeman worth his salt was eager to find the key piece of evidence which could convert these 'nearly' cases into prosecutions and imprisonments. This was the area where detection became a personal battle, with enemies who could be identified, defeated and put away for lengthy terms. These were the criminals who thumbed their metaphoric noses at the forces of order, the ones it always gave most satisfaction to confound.

But the DI drew the blank he had been half-expecting. It would be good if Lambert's snout came up with the missing piece in the legal jigsaw, but if he did, he would probably have to go into court as a prosecution witness. That was the point where things usually fell down: whatever the assurances of police protection, both the informer and those who sought to preserve him knew that no one could be guarded indefinitely against the violent retribution which was the inevitable reaction of the criminal world to grasses.

Rushton turned in desperation to those cases which the law had defined to its own satisfaction as manslaughter or suicide, but which the CID had found in some way more suspicious. These were inevitably local, for such suspicions were usually confined to word-of-mouth speculation, were sometimes, indeed, no more than the gossip of the section – for policemen in the canteen prattle and bitch about their work as intensively as those who follow other, less dramatic callings.

When Lambert arrived, he found his DI not staring at his computer but on the phone to a detective sergeant about a man who had fallen to his death from a warehouse platform in Tewkesbury some six months earlier. Rushton put down the phone so dolefully that there was no need to check that he had drawn yet another blank. Lambert tried not to sound smug as he said, with a glance at the shimmering green print on the computer monitor screen, 'So you haven't turned anything up yet, Chris?'

'Early days yet, sir.' But Rushton knew it was not. Three hours' concentrated effort had turned up nothing that he could even suggest might be significant. He acknowledged as much by giving Lambert a swift verbal summary of his morning's efforts. Even now, when he had worked with Lambert for four years and the brittle early days of that working relationship were far behind them, he felt a need to explain himself, to demonstrate how diligently and efficiently he had followed instructions, to justify himself and his early promotion to the rank of detective inspector.

Lambert looked quickly round the small modern office, hardly hearing Rushton's account of his morning: he took his industry and competence in such matters for granted nowadays. He was merely checking that he was alone before he said, 'Any further developments with Anne?'

Rushton, caught off guard by the personal question, looked up at him sharply. For an instant, his face had the openness and vulnerability of a child's. Then the sharp features closed again just as suddenly and he said, 'No, sir. The divorce is going ahead as agreed, I'm afraid.' There was a sudden shaft of pain, a flick of a cheek muscle as he said, 'We're just negotiating my access to Kirstie, now. They say it's better to get it agreed in advance than argue it out in court.'

'I suppose so.' Lambert thought of his own two-year-old grandchild, of what it would have meant to him all those years ago to lose his wife and his own toddlers, as he had so nearly done. His sudden sympathy for this man with whom he had so little in common was searing. He said awkwardly, 'Perhaps it's all for the best, Chris, in the long run.' Why did platitudes always take over when the heart was gripped by real emotion?

'So everyone keeps telling me. It's a great consolation.' The bitter sarcasm was as close as this conventional officer would ever come to insubordination.

'There's still time to begin again with someone else, you know.' Lambert knew as soon as he had said it that others must have already expressed the same unhelpful thought.

'Except that I don't want to.' The pain came out as almost a snarl, but Rushton did not apologize: perhaps he did not even notice. He took a deep breath, gestured angrily at the computer screen, and said, 'I've been over the usual ground without throwing up anything. Do you want me to start on the missing persons?'

Lambert thought for a moment about the vast, vague roll of those who for a thousand different reasons had left the ten thousand different environments which passed for 'home' at the end of this frenetic century. 'No. Not yet: there are far too many of them. I'll have to get more information out of Charlie Pegg, that's all. Always assuming he has it to give.'

It was the qualification an officer always made about his snouts: it was not unknown for CID men to initiate embarrassing wild goose chases on the basis of information which proved false. It was something every young DC feared, bringing upon him the wrath of a superior who was trying to control a budget and keep his men fresh for the real action. Lambert was long past that stage of his career, but old habits die hard. Perhaps also he wanted to show that as a superintendent he still thought and felt like the men he directed in major investigations.

But he was confident that Pegg knew something important. Over the years, he had developed a sort of trust with the little snout. The relationship between such a man and his detective contact must always be a peculiar one, with a streak of contempt as well as distrust involved. No one really admired a traitor, even when those he betrayed warranted no loyalty. But an understanding had built up over the years between the two of them, as information from the informant proved reliable and the discretion with which Lambert handled it maintained Pegg's security. Lambert had dealt intermittently with Pegg over ten years; there was now a sort of affection between them, though each still knew where he stood in this world of dangerous exchanges.

Lambert offered two thoughts before he left the room. 'I'll get on to the serious fraud office and find out if they're pursuing anything of interest on our local villains. And you'd better see if the drug squad at Bristol think any of our entrepreneurs are expanding into that field.'

It was no more than a slightly desperate attempt to supplement and complete Rushton's routine checking of the computerized information. There was no way he could have known at the time that this would lead to a man's death.

# 4

Charlie Pegg would have been flattered to know that he was occupying the thoughts of Superintendent Lambert. He did not have a high opinion of his own importance.

Like most grasses, Charlie had once been a petty crook. A little burglary, more opportunistic than planned, and not very professional. Then he had been drawn into a group, in the hope of greater pickings. But he had been no more than a fringe member, and it proved in retrospect to be a hopeless group, never attaining the status and menace it aspired to as a 'gang'. Their first venture had given them a hundred pounds from the till of an off licence. Their second had seen them caught and put away.

Two years Charlie had done, with the help of his remission; he had learned how to survive inside, by seeking out the most vicious men and making himself useful in tiny ways: even the craven fear which he scarcely troubled to disguise was useful to those whose chief instrument of domination was the threat of violence. It was in prison that he had discovered in himself the first talent he had identified in a drab life: the capacity to anticipate the desires of others and render small services. And in the last year of his porridge, he had learned how to work with wood, developing a skill which frequent truancies and nomadic schooling had hidden from him earlier.

When he had walked out between the granite towers of the Victorian prison, Charlie had sworn that he would never go back. Thousands of others looked up at those grim sentinels and swore the same oath, but very few of them were able to keep it. Charlie Pegg did.

No one would have expected it: his background and his intelligence scarcely seemed strong enough. Even his social worker had no great hopes for him. His success was achieved through two factors. Britain in the seventies was still the scene of a building boom: an active house-building industry meant that, unlike most of his fellow ex-cons, Charlie found employment fairly easily. His prison record meant that he never rose to the status of carpenter in charge of a site, but he kept regular employment as a chippy whilst the new estates rose around Cheltenham and Gloucester.

The second trump in his undistinguished hand was his wife. Amy Pegg was no great beauty, and she was neither more intelligent nor more far-seeing than her husband. But she was honest, and resolute that her husband should also be so. She took his money from him as he came into their council flat on a Friday, and gave him the amount which she thought would allow him to keep face in the pub without getting into mischief.

Charlie knew what she was doing, and approved it. He did not resent her budgeting for him; he rather liked it. It was the first time in his life that anyone had really shown a concern for his welfare and his future. He was proud of Amy; knowing what she was about, he became ever more determined not to let her down.

By the middle of the eighties, they had moved out of the deteriorating slab of council flats and into a small house of their own. Charlie modernized it, and Amy transformed the drab interior into a neat and bright little nest. The building industry began laying off thousands of men and the stream of new houses in which Charlie had whistled and planed his way to a modest prosperity almost dried up. But the recession scarcely affected the Peggs.

For Charlie, in the phrase Amy rolled out with increasing relish to her neighbours, 'went independent'. People who saw the way he had transformed his own house offered him work in theirs, cautiously at first, and confining themselves to tasks that were too small to offer to a regular builder. Planing doors to make them fit; making sash windows which had never opened for years glide smoothly up and down

24

their channels; putting up shelves for wives who had lost patience with husbands who had promised for years to get round to it very shortly.

Because his work was good and his prices were cheap, he was soon much in demand, and the jobs he was offered became more complex. He surprised himself sometimes by the quality of what he achieved. He did not take on major plumbing or construction jobs, because he did not have the equipment and he did not want to employ other staff – his confidence did not extend to that. But he became an expert on heating systems and domestic plumbing and all the other things he had watched from the sidelines during his days on the building sites.

George Lewis, the full-time porter at Old Mead Park, found himself besieged by requests for building modifications before the big block of flats had been open very long. The units might be luxuriously fitted, as the agent's selling brochure proclaimed, but the affluent people who moved in soon found ways to spend their money on numerous small improvements and adjustments to accommodate their individual modes of living.

It was natural in these circumstances that George should turn to Charlie Pegg. He and Charlie went way back – they had done their National Service together in Cyprus. As a result of that experience, George owed Charlie a debt they never spoke of, but which he was always looking to repay.

The porter's post at Old Mead Park gave him the chance to do that. He knew Pegg was a good enough workman for there to be no comebacks from his recommendation – indeed, the flat-owners were often pleased enough to slip Lewis a little something for his role as agent in securing this quiet and surprisingly effective little workman for them.

And this work fitted in very well with the other activity which Charlie Pegg had developed to supplement his income. He found himself in and out of most of the flats in Old Mead Park from time to time. Word went round that he was honest and trustworthy, so that the busy residents often left Charlie in the flats alone. They relied on George Lewis to provide whatever supervision and information were necessary; after all, what was the point of paying the salary of a full-time porter in an impressive dark-green uniform if he was not to be useful on occasions like this?

In one small way, Charlie Pegg was not as scrupulously honest as the occupants believed. Nothing was ever removed from these well-fitted homes. Nothing physical, that is: information was a different matter. It was surprising what letters and documents people left lying about. In time he extended that phrase to include unlocked drawers. Charlie read anything that he thought might be helpful to him, paying special attention to the increasing number of flats which had that intriguing modern phenomenon, the fax machine.

Sometimes messages actually printed themselves out before his fascinated eyes in the deserted rooms; it seemed to him not only technological magic but an open invitation to someone with his lively interest in what was going on amongst the entrepreneurial fraternity. In the case of one or two residents who became of special interest to him, he even ran through the messages left on the telephone answering machines, taking care to leave the tape exactly where it had been before he began to listen. There was rarely anything damning there, but it was useful to know who had been trying to contact one or two of the residents. People like James Berridge, for instance.

He did not tell Amy about this little adjunct to his working day. She might not have understood.

Charlie Pegg's squirrel-like and retentive mind stored away all he learned in Old Mead Park and all the other places he visited to deploy his carpenter's skills. And he used it to supplement the information, gossip and rumour he picked up in the more obvious hunting grounds for one of his peculiar calling. In the less reputable pubs of Gloucester and the surrounding area, the little snout kept up his connections with the criminal world. Many of the petty criminals who were the only ones he spoke with thought that he was still involved with crime, and he fostered that impression. As he never went to prison again, they gradually came to think of him as a shrewd operator, who associated with the big boys in crimes that went unsolved.

That irony appealed to Charlie Pegg, once he came belatedly to its recognition. He played up to his image a little; it was no more than an occasional knowing smile, never anything as blatant as a wink, but it was sufficient to convince the not very intelligent men with whom he conversed that Charlie Pegg moved with big fish and in deep and murky waters.

As indeed he did; but not in the way they thought. In discreet meetings in obscure places, Charlie passed on what he learned to John Lambert, the man who had been promoted in the years of their association from detective inspector to chief detective inspector and on to superintendent. Charlie was but dimly aware of these gradations in rank, but he took an obscure pride in the rise of his only police contact, the man who had given him help in finding the employment which enabled him to go straight all those years ago. Charlie even cherished the speculation that this rise might have been due in some small measure to the intelligence brought to him at infrequent intervals by his faithful snout. It was an illusion which Lambert was careful never to destroy.

Statistically, ten years is a long time for a grass to survive without broken bones or worse retribution. Charlie Pegg had already beaten the odds. Lambert knew just how heavy those odds were against his man, but he was careful not to remind him of them. A snout whose cover has been blown can never again be of any use to the forces of crime detection.

Charlie Pegg put together what he learned in his legitimate work with what he heard from his promptings during his evening visits to the pubs. He found it an interesting combination: each area tended to make more sense of the other, so that what might have remained obscure hardened into fact in his experienced hands. His income from informing had gone up steadily over the years, as his information had proved reliable and a steady stream of small crimes had been brought to court.

Now he was near to a big one. What he hoped to confirm in the next few days would be worth at least a grand, perhaps more. And he had read in the paper that some grasses might soon be put on a regular salary from the police budget. That would be respectability indeed, and a nice little earner on top of his regular work. Charlie Pegg, who was not given to flights of imagination, dreamed a little about the future.

For a little while, he forgot how dangerous an activity snouting could be.

# 5

Gabrielle Berridge would have been surprised to learn that Charles Pegg knew anything at all about her affairs.

When she spoke of him at all, it was to recommend his standard of work. Charlie had fitted a new waste disposal unit in her sink when she finally lost patience with the one originally fitted by the builders. She liked the kitchen to function as it should, though God knows she gave it little enough to do; the Berridges had no children and rarely ate in the flat together. And Charlie had made a good job of the cupboard which housed the water softener she had insisted on installing. James had been quite annoyed when she put Pegg into his study to build a cabinet for all the papers he left about, but she did not mind annoying James nowadays; sometimes she positively enjoyed it.

As far as Gabrielle was concerned, Pegg had been entirely satisfactory, not least because she had scarcely been aware of him. She arranged things so that he should do his work when she was out of the place, and thus cause as little disturbance as possible to her smooth routine of life.

This had been for years a rather sterile order, but now it had acquired a glamour, an unpredictability, even an occasional coarseness which she found unexpectedly exciting. These things came to her in the form of Ian Faraday. She would have thought at one time that she could never become an adultress; that was just another proof that you should never become too set in your ideas. As Ian had repeatedly emphasized to her.

She watched his broad back with a secret indulgent smile

29

as he sat up in bed and looked at his watch. 'It's time we were moving,' he said.

He did not sound at all convinced, and she liked that. Firm in getting her into bed, firm in bed, infirm about getting out, she had said to him an hour earlier. He encouraged her to talk dirty, and she was getting better at it. She would have been appalled to know that quiet little Charlie Pegg had heard some of the phone messages to which she had in due course responded.

She ran her index finger lightly up the undulations of his spine, then turned it so that her nail dug in lightly on the return journey. 'You don't mean you're not up to it any more, do you?' she said. 'Shot your bolt already, have you, big boy?' She stretched her lithe form suggestively beneath the hotel sheet, making sure at the same time that the silk still covered her. When you passed forty, it was safer for the curves to be felt than studied. Especially when you were fortunate enough to have a younger lover.

Ian Faraday sighed deeply, pretending reluctance, then drew in the sustenance of an enormous breath. 'Oh, all right, then! You talked me into it, you shameless, demanding woman.' He pulled her roughly on top of him; she giggled to disguise her embarrassment and delight as he pushed her limbs uncompromisingly into place.

The next fifteen minutes made her wonder how sound-proof the walls were between these hotel rooms; what a good idea those 'Do not disturb' cards were to hang on the door!

'Age cannot wither her, nor custom stale her infinite variety,' Ian said appreciatively as he eventually slid from beneath her. It was a dangerous line with an older woman, he knew, but he was confident of his ground with Gabrielle Berridge now.

She did not mind. She liked the way he quoted things at her. James had never done that, and it somehow lifted the affair on to a higher plane in her mind. And if Ian was going to identify her with Cleopatra, that wasn't a bad comparison. This time she let him leave her, stretching her sated limbs luxuriously as she listened to the shower and pictured him soaping his muscular torso.

In quieter moments such as this, she was prepared to acknowledge to herself that it added a little excitement that Ian was one of her husband's employees. Though she never put the idea into words, there was a strong sense of ironic satisfaction in the thought that the husband who had treated her with such contempt in their home should be supplanted not just by a man ten years his junior, but by someone whose money came from his own payroll.

Berridge had supplied the car in which they had driven here; and whichever of them paid for their room and their food, the money had ultimately come from James. There was a pleasing neatness about the revenge they were taking. She wondered if Ian ever felt the same neat satisfaction. He was shafting the boss and his wife at one and the same time: she must remember that daring indelicacy. It would please Ian, if she could come up with it at the right time.

Then, almost in the same thought, came the doubt which she was learning was never absent from the mistress's role. Was that what had attracted Ian Faraday to her in the first place? The knowledge that he was putting one over on the boss? He had said it wasn't, and she trusted him, but when you were four years older and your lover had the freedom to go elsewhere, you were bound to feel vulnerable.

At that moment, as if he knew her anxiety, he came out of the shower and paused to look down at her tenderly as he dried his hair. Then he sat on the bed and fondled her ink-black hair. 'Well, serpent of Old Nile, you've exercised your wiles again.'

'Yes, but don't expect me to leap out of a carpet at your feet. I'm not built for that any more. I reckon old Cleo must have been a mere slip of a girl when she pulled that one off.'

In truth, Gabrielle was slim enough, despite her statuesque delights. He ran his fingers from her hair, across her shoulder, down the inside of her arm, nestling his knuckles in the crook of her elbow joint. 'When are you going to make an honest man of me?' he said.

It was so much an answer to her anxiety that she had to

check with herself that she had said nothing to reveal it. She knew she should put him off the idea of marriage until it was more practicable. But she found it so delicious that she could not help toying with it, hoping that he would not allow her to dismiss it too quickly and sensibly. 'We can't do anything yet, Ian. James is not a man you can cross.'

Her tone belied the sense of her words, hoping he would find a way to refute the argument, though she knew there could be none. His smile disappeared; the little crooked frown she still found so attractive wrinkled his forehead beneath the brown hair. 'No. You're right about that.' He wondered if she knew just how ruthless her husband could be with his enemies; he had seen Berridge operating upon them at close quarters, as probably she had not. 'But it's only a matter of time. We'll find a way.'

'But how?' She knew how, but she wanted to hear him outline the glorious prospect again.

'I must get another job first. Before he knows anything about us, or he'll stop it. Stop me getting anything worthwhile, anywhere.' She put her hand quickly upon his, and he smiled at her. 'Don't worry, we'll manage it all right. I'd like something well away from here. I've still got contacts up in Manchester, but this damned recession means it's taking time. There are a hundred people after every decent job. But there are still people who rate me, you know, up there.' For a moment it was important to him that she understood his worth, in that wider world outside here, where she had never seen him.

'I know that, you silly man.' But she could not think how she was to show him that she knew it; she had never seen him with the team he managed. She simply knew that he would be competent and efficient, as he was as a lover. She dropped into the shaky northern accent she had learnt with the university dramatic society for their revue. 'But will they accept me up there, Willie Mossop, when there's trouble at t'mill?'

' 'Course they will, you daft ha'porth.' He had dropped his own Lancashire accent a long time ago, but he fell into it readily enough whenever he chose. He dropped it again immediately now, to show her this was serious. 'There are nice places to live, you know, in Yorkshire and Lancashire. It's not all grit and grime. We'll –'

She pressed her fingers softly upon his lips, enjoying the warm, damp mobility of them. 'I know there are, but I don't care where I live, so long as I'm with you. I'm not just a spoilt bitch who needs her comforts, you know. Well, only some comforts, anyway!' She took the towel and rubbed it softly around his groin, so that he sprang laughing away from her and began to climb awkwardly into his clothes.

She enjoyed watching him, as she enjoyed all his movements. He looked vulnerable now, giggling at her with one leg into his trousers like a gangling boy who is half-irritated and half-embarrassed by the scrutiny. She thought she could see in him the youth she had missed, and dwelt upon it, greedy for all of him, for those parts of his life that were still private from her, despite all their intimacies.

'Tell me again about the others,' she said. The words were out before she knew she had formed them. She was even more shocked that she should say such things at this moment than he was.

Ian stood, comically arrested in the act of zipping up his trousers, looking at her now with wide blue eyes and the hurt look of a schoolboy harshly accused. 'I thought we'd agreed not to raise that again,' he said. She could not tell whether he was annoyed or merely surprised.

'I'm sorry. I didn't mean to say it. I don't know what made me do it.' She reached out her hand for him, but his movements in the moments which followed were away from her: tucking his shirt hastily into the waistband of his trousers, pulling on his socks, fastening his tie, reaching out for his shoes and his jacket.

There was a pause before he gave her the rebuttal she realized now that she had been seeking. 'I told you. Those women didn't mean anything. Not compared with what I feel for you.' He came sulkily to a halt, aware that he was making the age-old protestations of the adulterer. He turned back to her with what was partly an appeal, partly a rebuke. 'I thought you already understood all that.'

'I have. I do.' She was miserable, feeling herself falling sheer and long from the heights she had so recently occupied, and dizzied with the misery which now threatened.

'I was divorced for four years before I met you, you know.' He was combing his hair, sounding apologetic and resentful when he wanted to do neither, watching her covertly through the mirror.

'I know. Of course I know. And I wouldn't want you to have lived like a monk.' She tried to convince herself of that by the force with which she said it, but it was his phrase, not hers, and it came to both of them as a quotation from an earlier, stale exchange. She said rather too abruptly, 'After all, you had to keep your hand in for the real thing when it came along.'

It was a brave attempt to restore the lightness between them. And it succeeded, in large measure. He recognized it for what it was, and immediately felt a pig for bridling a moment earlier. He went back to the bed and took her hand. 'You *are* different, you know. I didn't expect there would be anyone like you when – when I dabbled a little with those other women. They were there and available, so I didn't turn them away, that's all. But you make me wish I had.' At that moment, he almost believed himself.

Gabrielle smiled up at him. 'It's nice of you to say so. But you couldn't know you'd find me, could you? I'm just glad you did, that's all. You mustn't mind me being a neurotic old cow who wants her man to herself.'

'But you have me all –'

'Hush now!' She put her fingers lightly, laughingly on his lips, stilling his words, enjoying that small mastery over him. 'I know you'd like to be with me all the time. It's just that when you're not, strange fancies take over. I haven't much else to occupy my tiny mind, you see.' She beamed up at him, hoping their display of confidence would disguise the emptiness of her life without him and the desperate loneliness and insecurity which sometimes beset her in the gilded cage of the penthouse apartment at Old Mead Park. She wondered if it would be too late at forty-one to have a first baby. And how her new partner would react to that idea.

34

He put on the jacket of the business suit and completed the last move back into that working world of which she knew so little. When he kissed her briefly and left, she felt he was already a stranger.

She dressed slowly, fighting ineffectively against the bleakness which always stole over her when they had parted. Perhaps it was no more than the post-coital triste which her reading told her was common after the heights of passion. For in truth she was a novice in the emotions which are the setting for any stolen passion such as this.

James Berridge had been his wife's first lover. She was an attractive woman, with a suggestion of the gypsy girl beneath her well-bred, intelligent exterior, and in her two decades of unhappiness there had been many opportunities for her to take others. Yet now, after twenty years, Ian Faraday was her first excursion from the long-cold marital bed.

At forty-one, she was thrown off balance by her first heady experience of passionate sex and the disturbing flood-tide of emotions which came with it. It was both exciting and disturbing, not least because she did not fully understand what was happening to her. She spent the days when she could not see Ian wishing that she could be with him, wishing that like him she was free to make her own domestic arrangements. Like all lovers in her situation, she hated the secrecy shrouding a liaison which she yearned to present to the world in all its proud beauty.

Her resentment turned inevitably to the husband who was the unwitting obstacle to her desires. She frightened herself by the new intensity of her hatred for him. There were certainly times now when she wished him dead, and delicious intervals when she considered the vision of the simpler world in which that would leave her.

But what she found most disturbing were the moments when she discovered herself toying with the idea of killing him herself.

# 6

It had been a good day, Charlie Pegg decided. He had completed the installation of a new boiler in an Oldford garage in the morning, tested the system, and found it working perfectly. The staff had been full of praise as the heat seeped into their hangar-like workshop. The sense of accomplishment had given him great satisfaction in itself, for this had been the biggest heating job he had so far dared to tackle.

The fact that he had managed a revealing glimpse of a bank statement on the desk of the empty office was merely icing on the cake.

Late in the afternoon, he called to see his friend George Lewis, the porter at Old Mead Park. There was work for him in three of the flats, it seemed. Small jobs, more bother than they were worth in themselves, but sprats which in due course could net him mackerels. That was a pattern which had become familiar: customers who tested his work and found it satisfactory usually came back in due course with more challenging assignments. And Charlie noted with some satisfaction, as George Lewis showed him what was required, that he had not been in two of the flats before.

The third one was the luxurious penthouse of James and Gabrielle Berridge, where Mrs Berridge apparently wanted new locks on the drawers of her bureau. Charlie thought he could guess at the reason for that, but he asked Lewis to let him in for a moment to reconnoitre the work. The suggestion that they might enjoy a cup of tea and chinwag over old times in George's cosy little office near the entrance to the building sent the porter swiftly down in the lift; portering could be lonely work. Charlie Pegg found there were three

36

messages on the Berridges' answerphone tape. Then he spent an interesting three minutes in James Berridge's study.

Amy asked him about his day as she always did, and he told her everything he thought she should know. He knew his eyes were prejudiced, but he thought her as buxom and pretty as she had ever been. It seemed to him that Amy was one of the few women who improved with age, as her angularities disappeared beneath a pleasant plumpness. Perhaps it was contentment rather than all these mudpacks and face-lifts the Americans went in for that was the secret of retaining a woman's looks, he thought.

He went into the kitchen and put his arms round his wife's waist, leaning his chest lightly on her well-covered shoulders. 'Get on with you, Charlie!' she said automatically. Her low giggle became almost a purr of pleasure in the repetition of a ritual they both knew in its every detail.

The institution of marriage carries a multitude of ironies. It was at that very moment that Gabrielle Berridge was sitting combing her hair before the hotel mirror. She studied her abnormally bright eyes, her face still flushed with the warmth of her departed lover, and wondered whether there might be safe ways of disposing of her husband. And in her normally lucid mind, the distinction between a pleasant fantasy and a serious proposition became a little more blurred.

Charlie Pegg enjoyed his meal, as throughout the day he had known he would. Steak and kidney pie, fashioned with care and skill by his wife's experienced hands. Since his days in stir, Charlie could eat anything, but on his rare visits to restaurants he had never eaten anything as tasty as the meals served to him each day by the buxom Amy. There was fresh fruit salad to follow. Amy had been reading about diet in the glossy women's magazines she collected from the lady who employed her to clean twice a week; she did not have cream on her fruit, but she watched her husband pour a copious amount over his heaped dish with the indulgence of a mother.

She had lit a fire: it was still cold at nights, and they liked to sit by a real fire to watch the telly in the evenings, even though they could have relied on the central heating. They took their tea there now. Charlie said before they could settle too comfortably for the evening, 'I'll need to go out for a while later. See a man about a dog.' He was not sure what he meant by the old cliché, but it had become part of the ritual, an assurance that nothing abnormal or dangerous was involved.

'Do you have to, Charlie? You look tired. I bet you were humping heavy pipes about all morning.' This too was part of their conventions. She would never prevent him from going wherever he wanted to go, but she wanted him to know that she cared about his welfare, even as she indulged him.

'After your meals, I'm a giant refreshed.' He stretched his thin arms and his puny torso in a parody of Tarzan, and they both laughed at the incongruity of it. 'We'll watch *Coronation Street* together before I go. And I won't be late back.'

Amy sat down carefully with her tea, taking care not to spill a drop on the skirt that was newly released from its covering pinafore. 'If you are, I'll be suspecting you of running off with a blonde, so think on.' It was another line of their regular banter, which would have bored both of them but for the affection behind it.

'I'll just have to check, you see, that they don't need me for the darts team on Thursday. And I did tell George Lewis from Old Mead Park that I'd be in tonight, if he fancied a pint.'

They were his first lies, and he wished immediately that they had remained unspoken. They were not needed, for he never had to account for his movements to Amy nowadays, and they seemed a betrayal of the cosiness of the last hour. He pretended to immerse himself in the wildlife programme which preceded the *Street*, and they spoke little in the forty minutes which elapsed before the brass notes of the soap's signature tune announced the end of the episode and he rose rather reluctantly from the warm armchair.

He reversed his little van quietly out of the drive, hoping that the blaring of the television adverts would drown the sound of the engine: he would normally have walked the half mile to his local. At the end of the little cul-de-sac, he turned the vehicle away from that worthy hostelry and made his way swiftly towards the lights of Gloucester.

The industrial area was quiet at this time of night. He parked in the deep shade of the high brick wall of a warehouse. He had left the van in that vast cavern of darkness when he had come here before; he had no wish to advertise his presence in this place. He looked automatically around him after he had locked the car, but he was not expecting any human presence here, and he found none.

Satisfied, he turned towards his destination, which could not be more than two hundred yards away. He moved quickly, despite the shuffling gait which remained and was now a habit, an unconscious survival of those departed years when he had been subject to the whims of violent men. He did not see the figure which emerged from the side street when he had moved halfway to his goal; it followed him at a discreet distance.

The lights in the grubby pub were low, but the man he wanted to see was already there, waiting in the recess which they had chosen on other occasions because it was hidden from most eyes. Charlie bought two pints and set them on the small table with its rings from the bases of other glasses, its unemptied ashtray and smell of stale beer. Twenty years ago, he had done time with this man; in Charlie's imagination, his companion had the stigma of their cell still upon him. Indeed, it was not all imagination, for the man had spent eight of the intervening years in various of Her Britannic Majesty's prisons, and would doubtless return to at least one of them. He now had the grey face and bowed shoulders of a man who was so little in the open air that he found it an alien environment.

Charlie could not prevent a little surge of self-satisfaction when he considered his companion, with his grubby collar, black fingernails and downtrodden air. He transferred his mental thanks as usual to Amy, and determined with the same thought that he would not linger here longer than was strictly necessary. He might even consider giving up this aspect of his income altogether; there was no doubt that it was dangerous – and his building work was going from strength to strength.

But for the moment, he put himself out to be friendly. The man with him had had several drinks before he arrived. Charlie's experienced eye told him that it would not need much more lubrication to loosen his tongue. And they got on well enough. Charlie had done various small pieces of joinery in the man's council home, producing the same standard of work as he delivered to his richest clients. He had refused any financial payment and the man was absurdly grateful. He scarcely realized that he had made a different kind of payment, by means of the snippets of information he had volunteered to Charlie in his befuddled state.

Charlie Pegg's talent as an informer lay in fitting together scattered, apparently random scraps of information into a coherent whole. Once he had enough pieces of knowledge from his different sources and his own research, a lucid picture of what was afoot sprang out at him. The process gave him a certain intellectual satisfaction, though he would never have recognized it as that.

Tonight was such an occasion. Between gulps of beer, the man opposite him responded to his promptings with first a name, then, a pint and a half later, with a time. Charlie already had a fair idea of place. He gave no hint of his elation, though he realized that what he now knew could bring him the biggest police payment he had ever received. Instead, he went to buy his companion another beer.

On his way to the bar, he went briefly to the public phone, glancing swiftly around him before he dialled the number he knew by heart. He recognized the voice which answered, but did not identify either it or himself for any unauthorized listener to the line: that was the grass's code, and Superintendent John Lambert understood it as well as he at the other end of the line. Charlie said only, 'I have gathered now what you want to know. I'll meet you at the usual place.'

They were the sentences he had delivered on earlier occasions. Lambert knew the rules to protect his snout. He said simply, 'Tomorrow evening. Seven o'clock?'

'Yes.' Nothing save a slight excitement in Pegg's tone gave

a hint that this coup might be greater than any of his previous ones. He found himself tempted to give an inkling of its importance, but his discipline held and he rang off.

From behind a cloud of cigarette smoke ten yards away, the man who had followed him here watched Charlie's actions with interest, but made no effort to hear what he said. That might have alerted the quarry to his danger.

Charlie sipped the half of bitter he had contented himself with for the last half hour and concealed his impatience to be away, whilst the man on the other side of the small, round table drank his whisky and grew sentimental over old times. It would take a drunk to get nostalgic about the nick, thought Charlie. With that thought came a sudden revulsion for the man: perhaps he saw in him what he might so easily have become himself.

He was impatient to be away to Amy, but he did not mention her name to this man, as though she might be in some way tarnished by even so distant and indirect a connection with this world he had left behind. Or very nearly left behind; as he corrected himself, he determined again that he would now sever all connections. He would take whatever Lambert offered for this last and greatest of his deliveries, and then get out with his skin intact. Perhaps there would be enough to take Amy abroad, for the first time. Somewhere in the sun perhaps, during next winter's frosts; Amy always complained about the damp and the cold when the days were short.

Perhaps it was that thought which made him a little careless as he left the pub. He did not see the two men who followed, and though he glanced to the streets on either side of him, he did not look to his rear until he heard the sounds of their arrival at his heels.

It was still an hour before closing time, and the streets were quiet. The men were professionals, swift and efficient in the execution of their task. Pegg was down in an instant, falling with a cry which was scarcely more than a gasp of horror as he realized what was coming. He flung his hands behind his head and twisted into a foetal position, knees against his chest and head thrust deep into his breast, which might minimize the injuries in the beating he expected.

They gave him a blow or two, more to stun any impulse towards screaming than to damage him. For they intended worse than mere damage. The long, slim knife they used glinted briefly in the sliver of light from the streetlamp which was a good eighty yards behind them. The first thrust had gone home, right up to the hilt, before the man on the ground twisted one terrified eye to see it. It was plunged home three more times, searching for the ventricle in the left of the chest, before his assailants paused.

They were professionals, knowing that one thrust from a knife rarely killed, unless there was a lucky precision. They left nothing to chance. As their victim's sweater filled swiftly with blood over his thin chest, the man who had not stabbed him felt carefully for the vein in his neck, felt the pulse there slow, then stop, and nodded at his companion.

They left Charlie Pegg's body in the gutter, still a hundred yards and more from his van. It was another hour before Amy began to get anxious about him. By that time, the instrument of his death was at the bottom of the Severn, dropped there unhurriedly as his killers drove out of the city.

# 7

It was a night watchman, coming out of the back door of his warehouse in the first grey light, who found Charlie Pegg's body.

The blood had run five feet down the gutter, and there was a lot of it. The man, who had been anticipating a breakfast of thick bacon sandwiches and lots of tea, was suddenly no longer hungry. His first thought was that the men who had done this might still be around, his first impulse to run. Then, looking reluctantly again at the thing in the gutter, he saw that the blood was crusted and darkening at the edges of its gruesome flow. He accepted that this attack had probably taken place many hours previously and went back into the awakening factory to ring the police.

Lambert heard of Pegg's death while he was waiting to go into a divisional meeting about community policing and its implications for CID work. The sergeant who brought the message was unguarded enough to say, 'Well, I suppose he had it coming to him. Grasses always live dangerously, sir.'

'They are on our side, Sergeant.' Anyone who knew Lambert would have recognized danger in the quiet of his tone; those who worked closely with him would have known that the formal recognition of rank was often a prelude to an explosion from their superintendent. This man, preoccupied with his own concerns now that he had delivered the message from Oldford, picked up no warning.

'I suppose they are a necessary evil – a part of the police system. But no one can shed many tears over a grass, surely?'

'His wife will, in this case. And others too. Charlie Pegg was a good man. How many people of his background manage to

43

go straight when they've done time?' Lambert realized that he had never formulated these thoughts until now, even to himself.

The sergeant wondered why it was always his luck to run into the eccentrics of the force. Surely this grizzled senior officer should have acquired a little professional cynicism by now. He said stiffly, 'Sorry, sir. I didn't know you knew the man personally.' Lambert grunted, and the sergeant should have left it at that. Instead, he was unwise enough to venture, 'Not much chance of catching the blokes who did for a grass, though, is there? They'll have covered their tracks, and it won't be easy to find witnesses. No one likes a grass, whatever he might be like when he's not informing.'

'He's a man, Sergeant. Or he was. Now he's a man who has been brutally murdered. The worst crime of all. The one which will get all our attention; which will have to be solved if we're to stop the criminals running out of control.'

He went sourly into his meeting with the division's top brass, wondering how he had got into this exchange with an officer who was not under his control and whom he might never see again. His humour was not improved by the realization that there was something in what the man said: the chances of pinning down the shadowy men who had killed a snout were not high, because the degree of cooperation among the criminal fraternity, normally low, would no doubt be zero.

The tap was running steadily, sluicing the results of the scientific butchery which is a postmortem examination away over the stainless steel.

Lambert, resolutely avoiding the visual evidence by remaining in the office outside the laboratory, tried to shut his ears to the steady sound of the water. He was unsuccessful, for he found his mind filling with the images of gore and worse, swirling away into the drains. Cyril Burgess, wearing his green rubber boots and soiled cotton overall like the uniform of a soldier fresh from battle, wondered how best to exploit the delicacy of the superintendent's stomach for his own amusement.

'He bled a lot,' the pathologist said by way of conversational opening. 'Four or five pints gone before we ever got at him here. What the meat wagon brought in was an empty container, as far as blood was concerned.' He turned towards the entrance to his dissecting room with an invitational wave of his arm. 'He's still on the table: we can't sew him up until we've done more tests on the innards. I can show you if – '

'That isn't necessary!' The haste of Lambert's refusal brought a delighted smile from his tormentor. The superintendent was disgusted with himself for his weakness; he should have grown used to the abattoir aspects of the job in his uniformed days of twenty years and more ago. Yet somehow the worst of road accidents had never affected him as badly as the damage done to human bodies with full and malicious intent. He seemed to be becoming more squeamish as he got older. He strove for a professional question. 'How quickly did he lose all this blood? I mean, did it seep away gradually, or was there a sudden . . . ?' His words tailed away hopefully.

'Poured like a fountain, I should think. Positively gushed out,' said Burgess with relish. 'It does from the heart, you know, when they hit the main artery. Positively pumps out. But it would be much easier to show you – '

'I know how the heart works, thank you, Cyril,' said Lambert. 'You've explained it to me on previous occasions.'

'Really? Well, anyway, this one worked as it should. Case of "Who would have thought the old man to have had so much blood in him?" eh?' Burgess was an avid reader of detective fiction, who treasured an idea from his youth that no murder was complete without a quotation.

'Not so old,' said Lambert stolidly.

'No. About fifty, I'd say. Are you telling me that you knew him, John?' Burgess was suddenly put out, as if a new rule in the game had been invoked: if the dead man was known to Lambert, perhaps even a friend, his teasing would be in bad taste.

'I knew him, yes. I suppose he was about fifty.' It was a bleak reminder of his own mortality. He realized now that he had always thought of the nervous, shuffling little man as being older than him, when he must have been almost exactly the same age. He did not give any more details of the relationship to Burgess.

The pathologist became carefully professional. 'I can't give you a precise time of death, but he'd been dead for at least six hours before he was found, and probably rather longer. You can say with certainty that he was killed sometime before midnight.'

'Yes. We can probably pinpoint the time of death fairly accurately, now you've confirmed that. Apparently he was seen in the Star and Garter pub at around half past nine. We shall eventually find the man he was talking to there.'

The determination in Lambert's tone kept Burgess from any further attempt at humour. 'He'd eaten a meal of steak and kidney pie and two veg, followed by fruit salad and cream, approximately three hours before he died.'

'He'd been in the pub for some time. Was he drunk when he died?'

'No. A long way from it. He'd not had more than a pint of beer; maybe even a bit less than that.'

A meeting, then. And not just a convivial exchange about old times. Men like Charlie Pegg did not normally journey fifteen miles to spend hours over halves of bitter. Lambert said, 'How many men involved? Do the injuries suggest more than one?'

Burgess brightened at the prospect of being drawn into the investigation. He was fascinated by the processes of detection, though like most laymen he thought the business of investigation much more glamorous than it usually was. But at least his interest meant that he was prepared to speculate, in the hope of helping. The worst pathologists from any CID man's point of view were those who confined themselves stiffly to the statements they would deliver to a court.

He said now, 'It's impossible to say how many people killed him, John, from what's left in there. He wasn't beaten up – as you know, the boots and shoes as well as the fists of assailants can tell a story when a man is knocked about. There are a couple of bruises to the head – I think inflicted by gloved hands. But the only real damage is from the knife

46

wounds. The thrusts were repeated at short intervals, probably by the same person. But there were only four stab wounds, which suggests he stopped once he was certain that the wounds were fatal. There may have been two or three, perhaps even more men around him, but there's no evidence to show that.'

'Premeditated, rather than a row that went wrong.'

Burgess thought the words sounded like a statement rather than a question, but he responded nonetheless. 'It looks like it, John. You've seen a lot more violence than I have: we only get the worst in here. But if there's been an argument, I'd have expected to find other, more minor injuries, inflicted in the minutes before a quarrel escalated into a stabbing. Of course, with more and more people on hard drugs, one can never be certain.'

'I think this was a professional job, by hired men.' It was what he had thought from the first, but Lambert spoke the words reluctantly. It was the kind of killing that was most difficult to pin down, the kind anticipated by the sergeant at divisional headquarters to whom he had given such short shrift four hours earlier. He said to Burgess, volunteering him a little information in return for his attempts to help, 'Charlie Pegg spoke to me at half past nine. He thought he had something for me.'

It was the first time he had used a name for those pieces of dead meat that lay in the next room. And he had virtually said that the man was a police snout. Burgess felt absurdly touched by the confidence. He said, 'Everything about the wounds supports your view. A professional job. By professional cowards, of course. The victim appears to have been entirely defenceless.'

They were silent for a moment, trying to picture Pegg's last moments of life. Had he pleaded with his attackers? Had he recognized them? Had they confronted him with his supposed offence before they dispatched him? How quick and how painful had been his death? Then Burgess said, 'We've sent his clothes on to Forensic, of course. I doubt whether they'll tell you very much. There is one thing, though.' He paused, reluctant to revert to his earlier *Grand Guignol* details

47

now that he was aware that Lambert had been acquainted with this victim.

'Well?'

'The blood must have spouted from the man's chest. When his killer stabbed him on the second and third occasions, he must almost certainly have been splashed with substantial quantities of blood. The sleeves of whatever garment he was wearing will be heavily marked with blood. If you find that garment, it would be easy enough to match the samples.'

Lambert nodded and took his leave. He wondered as he drove away whether that garment had even now been destroyed.

Sergeant Bert Hook had spoken to Amy Pegg on a few previous occasions. She lived only half a mile from him, separated by a few fields and a straggling road of houses built at intervals over the last half century. The village bobby which still lurked beneath the CID man meant that Bert knew most of the people in his area.

This sporadic acquaintance was scant preparation for the task he now had. He shepherded her out of the mortuary, guided her to the white police car, watched her as she stowed herself, then put the seat belt carefully into place around her, as if she were either helplessly young or fragile with the extremity of age, instead of a vigorous woman of fifty. Shock took people like that; he had coped with it often enough to be an expert.

The CID section tended to use Bert to cope with the extremes of emotion, as Lambert had done now when he asked Hook to take Mrs Pegg to identify her husband. Policemen and policewomen have the same weaknesses as the rest of humanity. They mocked Bert for what they saw as an inappropriate sensitivity, for his predilection for the underdog in a world where they saw underdogs as more often than not the instruments of the crime they sought to control. Yet they were ready enough to exploit Hook's reputation for empathy when it meant that they could assign to him delicate tasks such as the first soundings of a bereaved spouse.

Routine has it that the next of kin are the first suspects in an unlawful killing, and the routine is such simply because statistics prove that it is justified. The first procedure is always to check the reactions to the death and the whereabouts at the time of the crime of those nearest to the deceased by ties of blood or marriage, even when as now the officer may be privately convinced that a spouse has no connection with the death.

'It was Charlie all right.' The woman in the back of the car spoke as though she were addressing the world at large rather than an individual, her eyes staring unseeingly at the hedges which flew past on each side. 'He was very – very white. Like paper. I thought for a moment it might be someone else.' Her words spoke of the split second of wild hope she had had by the corpse, but her voice was not the soft west country sound which Bert remembered; it had a dry rasp and a sporadic delivery. Like sweet bells jangled out of tune, thought Bert. He was doing literature in his Open University degree, and these comparisons sprang up now when he least expected them.

He did not say anything else until they were back in the neat little terraced house, thinking that she might talk more easily and be more reliable in her facts when she was on familiar ground. He looked at the neat, spotless room with its cottage suite and its flowered curtains and said awkwardly, 'You've got a lovely place here, Amy.' It was the first time he had ventured upon her first name. It was not entirely politeness; his own house, with two active boys of nine and eleven, never seemed to be tidy nowadays, except precariously, when they had gone to bed.

'Would you like a cup of tea?' She was standing in the middle of the room, still staring ahead as if addressing a group. It was convenient for policemen to behave as if their snouts did not have private lives, but the reality was confronting him now.

Hook said, 'Yes, I would. I very rarely say no to a cup of tea. But will you let me get it for us?'

She nodded, surprised by nothing after the awful shock which had filled her day. He sat her in a chair, made the

49

tea, decided which had been Charlie's favourite chair, and carefully avoided it. Perched awkwardly on the edge of the sofa, he waited until she had taken two gulps of the hot, sweet tea before he said, 'I have to ask you a few questions, Amy. So that we can get on with the business of finding out who did this to him, you see.' And so that I can officially eliminate you from the enquiry and leave you to your grief.

She nodded, turning her ravaged face directly towards him for the first time. 'He was giving you information, wasn't he? We never mentioned it, and he thought I knew nothing about it. But I knew.'

'I think he was, yes. But not to me. It was Superintendent Lambert he used to speak to.'

'Good man, he is. His wife taught my children, you know.' Bert's experience of bereavements made him used to such inconsequential statements. They were sometimes the first steps towards an accommodation with the world which had to go on.

'Did Charlie come home yesterday evening?'

'Yes. He had his meal here. We watched *Coronation Street* before he went out.' She sounded surprised that he should not know such things.

'So he left here at about eight.'

'Yes. Perhaps just after eight. He said he was just going to the local pub in the village.' Her face clouded with pain, whether at the deception or the thought that he might have been safe there he could not tell. 'He took the van. He wouldn't have done that to go down to the village.'

'We found his van, Amy. Near where he was found in Gloucester. He seems to have gone to a pub there. Have you any idea why he would have gone there rather than to the village?'

She thought for a minute. Her round face was distorted by grief, her eyes hollowed and sore with crying, but her forehead wrinkled now like a child's, as if she was showing him the honesty of her mental effort. 'No. I don't think it was anything to do with the business. He's gone independent now, you know, with his joinery building work.' She produced the familiar phrase with a little flash of pride, then

50

realized that the present tense would never again be appropriate for it. The tears they both hoped had finished gushed anew down the cheeks that were sore with their passage.

Hook said, 'And when did you expect him back, Amy?'

'About ten, or half past. But I didn't worry until after eleven. I thought he'd just got talking to his pals and stayed on.' She smiled bleakly. Even the weaknesses of a loved one became attractive with his passing.

Bert put the key question as gently as he could. 'But you didn't report him missing until this morning, Amy. Why was that?'

She did not seem to feel threatened. 'I don't know. I suppose I just didn't think anything horrible could happen to him. I went to bed eventually, sometime after twelve. I just thought he'd come creeping up to bed at some point during the night.' Again that picture seemed to give her a little painful pleasure.

'You didn't think he might be in danger?'

'No. Not at first, anyway. I was more worried when I looked out for him about midnight and saw the van was missing.'

'But you didn't give the station a ring, even then.' He looked at the telephone on the sideboard in the corner of the room, and she caught his glance and followed it.

'No. I – I didn't know who he'd gone to see, did I?'

Hook nodded, understanding the whole world of the Peggs' existence which lay beneath those simple words. Charlie was a jailbird, branded as such for ever in police eyes, even if his reformation had been achieved a long time ago now. And the process was two-way: he would never quite trust the police, and neither would his wife. There was a reluctance in Amy to associate with the forces which had put Charlie away all those years ago, even though it was she who had insisted that he should not transgress again. The instinctive fear of the police was the rule rather than the exception in Charlie Pegg's world.

'Can you think of anyone who would have wished to harm your husband, Amy?'

'No. Would it be someone he was – was grassing on?' She

51

brought out the word with an effort, facing for the first time the probable reason for his death.

'It's too early to say. But we think it might have been, yes.'

She shook her head sadly. 'I don't know anyone from that world. He kept it quite separate from his joinery work. He didn't even think I knew about it. Perhaps if I'd pressed him, he'd have given it up. But the money was useful, you see, until he got on his feet.'

'Of course it was. And he was bringing bad men to justice, Amy. Never forget that.' It was suddenly important to him that this decent woman should not blame herself for her husband's death.

'Men like the ones who have done this to him?'

'Yes. Men like that. Violent men, not petty thieves.'

She nodded, apparently satisfied on that score at least.

He checked that her daughter was on the way over, then left her washing the cups and saucers. But she came and stood on the doorstep as he climbed into the car. She looked like a woman seeing off a departing visitor conventionally. Wanting to say something by way of farewell, he could think only of, 'We'll get the men who did this to Charlie, Amy.' He immediately regretted it, for he knew their chances could not be high, and he hated false comforts.

But she called back, 'Make sure you do. And you'd better lock them away from me, Bert Hook!'

It was the first time he knew that she was aware of his name.

# 8

The routine of the enquiry produced very little on that first day. Several people had seen Pegg at the Star and Garter. One or two had seen him drinking with a man, perhaps for half an hour. No one could give a description of this companion. Or no one was willing to.

Lambert took Hook's report of his meeting with Amy Pegg and put it glumly together with the negative findings from the house-to-house and Scene-of-Crime teams. DI Rushton was running a computer search for similar killings when Lambert called him into the newly established incident room.

Charlie Pegg was getting the same treatment as any other murder victim. Lambert had set the centre up immediately as a visual reminder to his CID section that all deaths have to be investigated impartially, whatever the background of the victim, whatever the possibilities of success. Charlie Pegg would have been surprised and immensely flattered to know that his death had been accorded this measure of importance.

In truth, there was little in the room yet. The clothes which would eventually be carefully bagged to appear as exhibits in court were still with Forensic. The files of interview evidence which would in due course fatten to an alarming volume, even in a case like this, had scarcely been opened. Some enlarged photographs of the corpse and the place where it had been found had been pinned on a sheet of plasterboard, but there was little else to suggest that this was a murder room.

Rushton gave them a résumé of the largely negative findings he had collated so far. He said, 'The only interesting thing is that the landlord thought he saw Pegg making a phone call last night. It would be useful to know whom he was trying to contact.'

Lambert smiled grimly. 'Not all that interesting, I'm afraid, Chris. It was me. He got through and we arranged a meeting – that should have been in our usual place tonight.'

'Any idea what he wanted to talk about?'

The superintendent shook his head ruefully. 'He had information about someone. Some job that was coming up, I expect. He never rang me without it. But we didn't even exchange our own names on the phone, let alone any facts. He was too well versed in his trade for that.'

But his knowledge didn't save him, they all thought.

Hook said, 'Haven't you any idea, sir, from previous contacts?' There was almost a superstition about the exchange: even now, when the man was dead, neither inspector nor sergeant mentioned the place where the snout would have met Lambert, nor speculated about the men whom he might have been planning to expose. They would wait for Lambert to give the lead. Informing was a curious business, and the danger of it had just been vividly underlined.

Lambert said, 'I have ideas, yes. Proof is going to be very difficult, if the man responsible is the one I suspect. Jim Berridge won't have done this himself.' He looked at the picture of the corpse, with its long trail of dark blood running away down the gutter, whilst the other two pondered the name he had given them. 'There is one thing already from the pathologist. This wasn't a beating-up that went wrong, a warning-off that got out of hand. The man or men who did this came with a knife to kill Pegg. That was their intention from the start.'

Rushton said, 'I think you're right. And I see what you mean. Most grasses get a nasty attack of GBH. To stop their tricks and warn off anyone else who might be thinking of doing the same. Not many of them are actually killed, even today.'

'That's what I'm thinking. Even now, not many criminals are prepared to contemplate homicide, if they can avoid it. They know that if it goes wrong there is an automatic life sentence. So they don't kill, unless they are desperate, or

54

stupid. The way this killing was achieved shows that these men were neither. I think that we are looking at men in the big league, confident and ruthless. And satisfied that we won't be able to pin this on them, even if we suspect – even if we know – who they are.'

Neither of his listeners offered an opinion on that. If they thought the confidence of these known purveyors of violence was justified, they knew Lambert too well to say so. Instead, Hook said, 'Amy Pegg gave me Charlie's little red book.' He handed over a small, rather battered red notebook, of the kind that could be bought in any stationery shop. 'It's pretty cryptic, as you would no doubt expect. It might mean more to you than to me, as you'd been his contact for so many years.'

Lambert thumbed quickly through a few pages. The only things which were definite were a few dates. People were referred to by no more than an initial. He wondered if even those were genuine, or whether they represented some kind of code. But he saw a note on the last of the pages the little man had used which said, 'Ring L.' and realized with a curious cold thrill that the entry referred to himself. He said, 'I'll go through this later. It might give some idea of the people we're after, but I'm pretty sure there won't be anything that would be very convincing as legal evidence. Charlie Pegg was too cagey to leave much around for his enemies.'

On the table behind them, the telephone bleeped, as if giving a signal to kick-start the machinery of the investigation into life. Rushton had the receiver in his hand before it had the chance to sound again. He gave little more than two affirmative grunts to punctuate his listening.

As he put the phone down, he said to the two who waited, 'They've got the man Pegg spoke to in the pub last night. They're bringing him in now.'

Lambert spent an hour poring over the late Charlie Pegg's little red book. It was an irritating document, full of suggestion but delivering very little concrete information. At the end of the hour, he went off to see the one person who had actually been named in the book.

George Lewis came out to meet him from the porter's office when Lambert parked his big old Vauxhall in the section reserved for visitors to Old Mead Park. It was impossible to tell from his bearing whether he had been expecting a police visit; perhaps he felt it was his duty to show a presence to all visitors to the block of luxury flats. As the end of the century approaches, the defence of riches is eternal vigilance; Lewis had been made aware by the trustees when he was appointed that he was to be the major and most visible element in that vigilance.

He knew who Lambert was, though they had never met previously. And he seemed to have heard about Pegg's murder, for he nodded curtly when the superintendent told him why he had come, then took him swiftly into the warm little cubicle which was his private domain against the comings and goings of a busy world.

The room had a radiator, which was heated by the boiler which warmed the public sections of the block, so that there was no need for a fireplace in the room. If the room had a focal point, it was no more than the small cupboard on which stood an electric kettle and a tray with assorted mugs. There was a coloured plan of the flats on the wall above this, an adaptation of the architect's original drawings, which showed the disposition and ownership of the apartments on the different floors. Lewis had long since ceased to need it, but it came in useful occasionally for directing visitors arriving in the place for the first time. Beside it there were the small red lights of a complicated electronic alarm system, which would sound in here as well as elsewhere if any of the rooms around and above him were entered illegally. George considered its presence here was a visual deterrent to any thief who might come in with the idea of establishing his bearings; certainly there had been little trouble in the two years since the flats had been completed.

Lambert, studying the plan and the alarm system surreptitiously, could have given him another opinion about that, but that was not why he was here. He said, 'You knew Charlie Pegg? Your name is in his book of notes.'

'Yes, I knew him. Pretty well.' For a moment, it seemed

56

that Lewis was going to say something more. Then the kettle came to the boil and he poured the scalding water carefully into the teapot. 'I was able to put him in the way of some work here, when he was getting going on his own.'

'And his work was satisfactory?'

'More than that. Charlie was the best. He knew what he was about, and he was prepared to spend the time, even if it took longer than he had thought it would when he gave his price.'

Lewis had the air of a man who had sponsored a protégé and is proud of the results. Lambert was reminded for a moment of an ageing impresario he had interviewed years earlier, who had claimed to have given Tony Hancock his first billing. He wondered how best to phrase his next enquiry. 'You were quite happy to let him work in the flats on his own?'

Lewis's eyes narrowed for a moment; then he decided to smile rather than take offence on his friend's behalf. 'I knew about Charlie's record, if that's what you're hinting at. Between you and me, I even did the odd bit of thieving with him myself, for about six months after we came out of the army. Before I got married and saw the light.' He looked at Lambert; rather to his disappointment, the superintendent's face registered no surprise.

'But Charlie'd been going straight for a long time. If I hadn't known he was safe, I'd never have recommended him – more than my job's worth. I went in with him at first, but I'd have done that with any workmen who came, if the residents were out. And Charlie would never have let me down. We go back a long way, you know.'

Lambert, thinking of the cryptic entries in that little red book, suspected that there were other, more intangible things than property which might have been at risk from Pegg's observant presence. 'How many of the residents did Charlie work for?'

George Lewis looked at him suspiciously. 'Six, perhaps seven.' He glanced up at the plan on the wall. 'I could give you a list. But I told you, Charlie would never have –'

'Charlie Pegg was murdered, Mr Lewis. All I want to do is to find out who killed him.'

Lewis looked at him for a moment as if he did not believe that, as if he was seeking for some other, more convincing motive for this questioning. Then he nodded, pushing a mug of tea into the hands of the seated Lambert. 'All right. I want that too – more than you could possibly realize.'

There was such feeling on the last phrase that this time Lambert did not let it go. 'Perhaps you should tell me about that. I go back quite a long way with Charlie myself.'

Lewis said, 'I know. Charlie told me how you helped to get him going with a job when he came out of the nick.' But not, presumably, that he had acted for ten years as a snout: Lewis would surely have mentioned that relationship, had he known of it. 'But I knew him much longer than that. As I said, we were in the army together, for National Service.'

Lambert smiled. 'They caught me for that, too. It seems a vanished world, now.'

'It is, more's the pity.' Lewis frowned, and Lambert thought he was about to go into the ritual denunciation of the lack of discipline among the present generation of adolescents. Instead, he said unexpectedly, 'But National Service was a waste of time, for most of the two years. Taught a lot of people how to skive, even if their boots shone.'

Lewis seemed about to develop a philosophical strain which would have been just as much of a diversion as the calls for square-bashing and blind obedience which the superintendent had been expecting, so he tried a little desperately to bring the conversation back towards the dead man. 'Did you get abroad, or were you stuck in barracks here?'

Lewis looked at him as if he were grateful for the correction. He took a reminiscent pull at his mug of tea, for all the world as if he had been relaxing in some far-off NAAFI. 'We were in Cyprus, Charlie and I. He was a good lad. Younger than me, but he knew what was what.'

There was plainly more to come. Lambert sought for a phrase to grease the machinery of articulation. 'That would be during the troubles in Cyprus, I suppose.'

'Not 'arf. Makarios was making more trouble every week

with the politicians, and Colonel bloody Grivas was organizing EOKA to gun down the troops.' The old names, half-forgotten even by Lambert, sprang to his lips with the freshness of a grievance remembered. He pushed the biscuit tin at Lambert, scarcely noticed his refusal, and said quietly, 'He saved my life, you know, did Charlie.'

It was so unexpected, and the dead Pegg was so much the opposite of a heroic figure in his appearance and bearing, that Lambert must have shown his surprise. Lewis banged the tin back on to the top of its cupboard with a clang of irritation and said, 'I'm not exaggerating. It's no more and no less than the truth. We were different then, you know, all of us.'

It was the perennial appeal of ageing men to be remembered in the pride of their youth. This time Lambert responded immediately. 'We were indeed, George. Tell me about it, then.'

'We ended up on patrols in the hills, looking for the terrorists who were waging the war the politicians weren't allowing us to fight. I know not very many were killed overall: the brasshats kept telling us that. But those who were killed were shot in the back. Those EOKA buggers knew their way round those hills and we didn't – we were sitting ducks, looking round the rocks and trying not to shit ourselves.' Lewis, carried back to the attitudes of over thirty years before, did not even notice phrases he had long since abandoned in his present life.

'And they nearly knocked you off?'

'Knocked me off. Not Charlie. Yes, the buggers nearly got me. I was the lancejack in charge – there were only four of us; we'd started off as just a roadblock. But there was activity in the foothills just above the road, and we were ordered in by radio. As the NCO, I was at the front of the four, waving my rifle and trying to look like John Wayne. We were about to turn back and report that we'd found nothing when the incident occurred.'

He had fallen back into the military phrase he had thought long forgotten, and Lambert responded in kind. 'You came under fire?'

'Yes. But there were no casualties.' This time Lewis gave a tiny, mirthless smile in acknowledgement of the jargon. 'But that was due to little Charlie Pegg: he was only eighteen then. One of the bloody guerrillas jumped out from behind a boulder, not more than fifteen yards away. He was slightly behind me, and I never saw him. But Charlie did.' Lewis, experiencing again the dust and the fear of that desperate moment half a lifetime behind him, could not keep his voice steady.

Lambert was for a moment caught up in the distant drama. 'Did Charlie shoot the man?'

'No.' Lewis grinned at the recognition. 'He said he'd have missed, if he'd tried. He shouted and threw himself on top of me, knocking me flat as the man fired his rifle. Our other two men took a pot shot at the guerrilla, but he was away like a monkey over the rocks. Fortunately, he was on his own – we thought at first we'd walked into an ambush.'

'And neither of you was hit?'

'No. But I would have been, for sure. The bullet took a chip out of the rock I'd had my hand on. I kept the bit of stone. If it hadn't been for Charlie Pegg . . .'

George Lewis shrugged expressively, a small, balding man in a safe, warm room and a safe, cosy job, recalling a moment of drama which seemed at that moment to have happened to a wholly different man in a wholly different world. 'Charlie could easily have been killed himself, of course, in the act of saving me. I've thought about it a lot, over the years.'

Lambert said, 'Did he get an award?' It seemed the line which was needed from him to complete the tale satisfactorily.

'Did he buggery! I reported it all, but all they did was query the wisdom of the military action I had taken. Then they said there was no senior rank to witness Charlie's act of gallantry, so it couldn't be officially rewarded. If you ask me, the four of us should never have been ordered to go off at random like that, and the CO didn't want it officially examined.'

'You could be right at that,' said Lambert. Lewis accepted

the words as the assurance of one old sweat to another, and seemed content that it should conclude his account of times past and favours owed. Lambert produced the little red book and succeeded in confirming several of the initials there as belonging to owners of apartments in Old Mead Park. He did not show Lewis the enigmatic entries alongside the initials, lest his faith in his dead friend's integrity should be tarnished.

Instead, he said, 'What do you know about James Berridge, who has the penthouse apartment, George?'

Lewis looked automatically at the door, checking that they were shut in where none could hear them. 'I know he's a villain. Though I wouldn't say so to anyone but you. Charlie let that slip: he never said much, but I think he wanted me to be on my guard against him.'

Lambert nodded, taking a swift decision to venture a little information in the hope of greater returns. 'He might be involved in Charlie's death, George. But not directly: he certainly didn't kill him himself. Keep your eyes open for us. But please don't do any more than just that. Leave the risk-taking to us. We're paid for it.'

George Lewis nodded, then buttoned the jacket of his uniform and opened the door, dropping back into his professional persona after the confidences of the last half hour. He accompanied the superintendent to his car, assuring him that he would contact him if he saw anything that might be of relevance to the investigation. As Lambert climbed stiffly into the big Vauxhall, Lewis said, 'Get the man who killed old Charlie, Mr Lambert. And just make sure I don't get there first.'

He was a slight figure, almost comic in his bravado. But his vehemence gave him dignity. Lambert retained the image of the short figure standing at attention long after it had disappeared from his rear-view mirror.

Back at Oldford CID, the man with whom Charlie Pegg had had his last conversation was in trouble.

In the small, windowless interview room, Joey Jackson was no match for Rushton and Hook. He said without conviction, 'You don't want me – I've nothing to tell you.' It was the view he had been repeating ever since the uniformed men had bundled him into a car as he came out of the betting shop in Gloucester.

'We shall be the judge of that.' Rushton was almost puritanical in his detachment; even his distaste for this pathetic specimen was under strict control. 'I ask you again, and this time consider your answer carefully: what were you talking about last night with Charlie Pegg?'

'Nothing. Well, not nothing, but nothing important. I don't remember much – I got a bit drunk, you see.' His lips twisted, but even the sickly, apologetic grin he was searching for could not find its way to them.

Hook could smell the fear upon him. It was, he supposed, an amalgam of bad breath, dirt and sweat, and in that sense had a physical explanation. But it was a smell he had known before, and always from men who were deeply afraid. As if taking up that thought, the man on the other side of the small table said, 'You could get me killed, if they knew I was in here talking to you.'

'So who are "they", Joey?'

'I don't know. The men who killed Charlie.'

Rushton eased back for a moment, studying his man. 'And why did these men you don't know kill Charlie?'

Jackson glanced automatically from side to side, as if seeking the relief he knew could not possibly be there. His face was white, with the damp film of tension like oil upon it. 'I've only tumbled to it today. Charlie was a grass, wasn't he?'

'Was he, Joey? And what was he doing talking to you, then?'

Jackson licked grey lips. He was only realizing now how subtly Pegg had been probing him last night. His panic deepened; he could not remember how much he had told the insistent little man. He was trying to recall how much he had drunk. No wonder Charlie had been so generous! 'He must have been trying to get information out of me, I suppose.' Jackson dashed his lank hair away from his left eye in an automatic gesture, then found that there was no hair there. But he felt the wetness from his temple on his knuckles.

Rushton eased forward now, until his face was no more than a foot from his prey. 'Now we're getting somewhere, at last. What information, Joey?'

'I don't know. I can't — you're asking me to grass —'

'I'm asking you nothing, Jackson. I'm telling you. You're going to tell us what you told Pegg, however long it takes. This is a murder enquiry, and you're right in the middle of it, mate!'

'I — I want a lawyer.'

It was said without conviction, and it brought only a harsh laugh from Rushton. 'You can have one when you're under arrest. Meantime, you're merely helping us with our enquiries. As a good citizen should. Of course, you're free to go at any time. We'll drop you off: somewhere round the pub where you were talking to Charlie Pegg last night. With a prominent police escort, and very obvious and noisy thanks for all the help you've given us.'

Jackson's nostrils flared almost as wide as his eyes. He flung his head back as if he had been struck, then eased his thin buttocks back along the seat of his chair. He felt as if any touch from this awful detective inspector would brand him for ever as an informer. 'You can't do that. I wouldn't last five minutes if they even thought —'

'There is an alternative, of course, Joey. You can tell us everything you told Charlie Pegg last night, and let us make our own deductions. And we can let you go quietly, at some place you might care to suggest as being safe for you. Because we are always anxious to help those who behave as good citizens should.'

Joey Jackson looked from the face of his tormentor to the weatherbeaten countenance of the sergeant beside him who had hardly spoken. He was trying desperately to think, to spot the pitfalls, to discover any way out of the appalling situation in which he had landed himself for the sake of a few free drinks. Bert Hook was aware that this was his moment, though his face gave no sign of it. He said gently, 'We need to know, Joey. And you need to tell us, you see. You don't want to be here all day, with villains out there wondering what you're doing.'

Jackson wanted to bury his face in his hands, to shut out those experienced, expectant faces, to shut out the featureless green walls of the room behind them, to give himself time to think. But his maleness would not allow him such a gesture of despair and submission, even in this extremity. Instead, he looked at the scratched surface of the table and said, 'Have you got a fag?'

It was the acknowledgement that he was going to co-operate. Rushton said, 'In a few minutes, when you've talked to us. If you talk properly, this could be all over in a few minutes.'

Jackson said, 'I can't remember much that we said. He was clever, Charlie – I can see that now. And I was really pissed, by the time we finished talking.' He was suddenly anxious that they should believe him.

'I expect he didn't say a lot. Kept you talking, most of the time.' Hook had known Pegg, a little; more important, he was experienced in the ways of the snout, treading dangerous ground on the edge of the underworld.

Jackson was grateful for the understanding. 'Yes, he did. I run a little transport business, as you know, with my own Transit van. He asked me who I'd been working for, over the last few weeks.'

'And where?'

'Yes.' Jackson, racking his brain for the recall, was surprised at the range of what Pegg had covered, making casual, apparently friendly enquiries about the welfare of his business while the drinks came faster and faster. 'He must have picked up most of my calls over the last couple of months.'

'And the next couple?'

Jackson was becoming more uncomfortable by the moment as his recall of the conversation improved. 'Yes. The next month or so, anyway.'

Rushton said, 'You operate for some pretty dodgy people, Joey.'

'I take what business I can. I have to. But nothing illegal – not knowingly.'

'Ignorance is no defence in law, Joey. But all we're interested in at the moment is the names you talked about to Charlie. Especially any in which he seemed particularly interested.'

Jackson was pathetically anxious to help now. Some interesting names tumbled out of his drink-fractured memory. The CID men did not prompt him. They had almost given up hope of hearing the name which interested them most when he eventually delivered it. 'There was one job which was too big for me which Charlie seemed particularly interested in. I only have the one vehicle, you see, and this was going to need two or three.'

'And who was the man who wanted to use you for that?' Rushton's professional indifference should have been recorded for an interrogation training tape.

'It was for James Berridge. I don't expect you know him.'

# 9

The name Berridge had several interesting entries in a file on DI Rushton's computer, though there was no criminal record. Jim Berridge, as he boasted privately to the small circle of his favoured companions, had won hands down in his contests with the police: he had never even been taken to court.

So far, said Chris Rushton grimly to himself, as he checked the file. So far.

The entries on Berridge threw up other names, the names of men who might well have been involved in the killing of Charlie Pegg. Hard men, who took no prisoners and covered their tracks with automatic expertise. Rushton discussed these names with Lambert, agreed with him that they must be interviewed. Rushton had old scores to settle with them from his early days in CID; he asked that he might see them himself. And he asked if he might take Bert Hook with him.

Lambert was both astonished and delighted, though he took care to reveal neither emotion. Rushton, despite his own promotion to detective inspector, had always resented the close relationship between Lambert and Hook. He knew that Bert had passed up the chance of becoming an inspector to remain a sergeant, and in a profession where the progress of one's peers is jealously monitored, integrity is almost resented, as if it were in some way a comment on the ambitions of others.

Lambert had long known the investigative skills which lay beneath Hook's rubicund village-bobby exterior. To find the younger man now actively seeking Bert's assistance could only be a strengthening of the team. And the unshakeable Hook would be a useful counterbalance to the new intensity he thought he saw rising in Rushton since the departure of his wife and daughter. A concentration on work could benefit both the man and the job after a woman had left, but it could sometimes tumble into disaster if a proper perspective disappeared with the increasing determination to succeed. Too many frustrated policemen were taking short cuts to get convictions these days.

Rushton and Hook found the men they wanted in the Curvy Cats night club in Bristol. They made no attempt to evade police questioning, but they were a very different proposition from feeble Joey Jackson.

At two-thirty in the afternoon, the place still smelt of stale drink and cigarette smoke from the night before. A peroxide blonde in a stained lurex dress was rehearsing with a pianist who looked as if he would rather be anywhere but here; the uncertainty of her vocal line echoed back from the midnight-blue walls which rose high above the sparse lighting to an invisible ceiling.

Rushton said, 'We have things to ask you two. We can do it here, or at the station.'

The men did not even look at each other. Perhaps they had expected this visit; if so, they were far too experienced to reveal the fact. The bigger of the two said, 'Going to arrest us, are you?' He did not even take the trouble to be contemptuous: his tone was almost polite, as if he was merely seeking information rather than asserting his rights.

He was a large man, an inch taller than Rushton's six feet, and probably three stones heavier. That weight was not fat, but muscle. He had black trousers, a black T-shirt, and a sleeveless black leather jerkin on top of it. Beside him, leaning back with him against the bar, his companion might well have been a slightly smaller reproduction; he wore the same clothes, which made them look like a uniform. Perhaps that was the effect they aimed at. They were a formidable pair, and the similarity contributed to their air of menace.

Rushton looked round the place. A girl was cleaning the

marble dancing floor with a mop and bucket, lethargically. Perhaps she was hoping to hear their conversation, but she gave no evidence that she could be interested by anything. Behind the bar against which the two large men lounged, a man was wiping glasses and stacking them on a shelf. Rushton would have liked to go to some smaller, more private room, where he could study the faces of these men as he spoke to them, but he was determined not to allow them the pleasure of refusing such a request.

Instead, he said, 'You work here?'

'Yes.'

'In what capacity?'

The larger man allowed himself a small smile. 'We maintain order in the evenings. You wouldn't believe how stroppy some members of the public can get. And of course there's never a policeman around when you want one. We also give a little help during the day, when things need moving around.'

'You act as bouncers, in fact.'

'We do indeed, Mr Rushton.' He grinned at his companion, who returned the smile like a diabolic mirror.

'Doing considerable physical damage on occasions, no doubt.'

The two formidable pairs of shoulders shrugged in unison. 'We do no more than is necessary. Some of the punters get quite obstreperous. It's the drink, you know: it's a terrible thing!' He let his voice rise on this condemnation, mimicking one of the drag performers who occasionally pranced on the tiny raised podium five yards to his right. It was another way of mocking his questioner.

Rushton found it frustrating that in this light he could not even see the colour of the man's eyes. He was fighting not to show that he was ruffled. He said abruptly, 'Where were you between ten and eleven o'clock last night?'

The bigger man raised his eyebrows a fraction, turning to his companion with an elaborate show of earnest concern. 'We must have been here, Walter, as usual, I suppose. Working our little socks off to earn an honest living.' The other man nodded vigorously, allowing himself the smile his companion had eschewed. Sturley turned back to Rushton and said, 'Why, did we miss something interesting elsewhere, Inspector?'

His elocution was that of a public schoolboy, the words being enunciated as carefully as they were chosen. It was disconcerting, and again Rushton had to fight to conceal the fact. Hard men, who sold their violence to the highest bidder in an increasingly buoyant market, should speak like the dangerous morons they were, stringing sentences together with difficulty. Sometimes it was even possible to intimidate their fuddled minds with words. But this man seemed to enjoy them, taking advantage of a secure alibi to taunt them with the phrases of his confidence.

The truth was that William Sturley had a predilection for violence which education had not been able to control. He had enjoyed being the school bully, the successful centre of flailing fisticuffs whenever he could provoke resistance in those weaker than himself. Nowadays, he realized that he had even enjoyed the punishment which his actions had occasionally brought upon himself. In adult life, he had never been able to skirt those situations which offered the possibilities of brutality with him in control. That had held him back from the subtler and richer villainies that his intelligence might have devised.

But he made a lucrative living from providing the supporting violence for others who had pursued those paths. Lucrative, because he was swift, efficient and ruthless. And because he was prepared even to kill, when others, even among the hard men, shrank from this ultimate violence and the penalties detection might carry. Sturley enjoyed his work; he thought that was probably why he was so successful in it. And he was not about to be undermined now by any jumped-up Plod in plain clothes.

Rushton said sourly, 'No doubt there are people who will vouch for your presence here last night.'

'No doubt. It wouldn't be difficult to find them. Because that's where we were, you see. We were on duty, together. We're a good team, Walter and I.' They did not even need to look at each other to coordinate their smiles as they lounged back against the bar, confident, full of menace.

Hook, who had been surveying the inflated drink prices displayed on a tiny notice on the wall behind the bar, spoke for the first time. 'Early in the evening, that would be, for this place.' It seemed at first an inconsequential thought. He delivered it quietly, making it a statement rather than a question; his Gloucestershire accent, slight but without any attempt at disguise, struck an incongruously rustic note in this urban sink.

The unexpected accent, from a man they had never expected to speak, might have been what scratched for the first time at the veneer of urbanity the two gorillas had adopted. The shorter one, as if taking his cue to reply to the lower-ranked policeman, said, 'Yeah, it's quiet in here until after the pubs close. Most of our trouble comes after midnight, when we get it.' He ground his massive right fist against his other palm, then looked down and hastily desisted, like a large schoolboy caught in a telltale gesture. He eased forward as he said aggressively, 'What of it?'

Bert took his time, catching the scent of pickled onions on the man's breath, studying him dispassionately, as if he had given something vital away. This was the man to go for in the pair, he decided. 'It's interesting, that's all. It would have been quite possible to slip out for an hour, an hour and a half even, without being missed, and still be back for the peak-period for bouncing.'

'We didn't. Ask any of the people around here.'

'We may do, if we have the time. But I've no doubt they'll support you. We may in due course ask some of the punters, of course. And members of the public from the surrounding streets, who may have seen you moving out of the car park. And the local beat bobby. And the traffic police on the M5 and the A38. There are all kinds of possibilities, when a murder investigation allows us to cast a wide enough net.'

'Murder?' The word brought its reaction, even here. Sturley would have liked to prevent his companion speaking. He would even intervene to do so, if it got sticky, but he did not see how it could. He glanced at Rushton. The girl stopped singing, and somewhere to their left another light came on; Sturley and Rushton held each other's eyes as the two shorter men at their elbows went on with their exchange.

Hook said, 'Murder. Of Charles Robert Pegg. Near the Star and Garter in Gloucester. But you know all about that.'

Sturley decided it was time to intervene. 'Prove it!' he snapped. The urgency of it was as much a warning to his colleague to shut up as a response to Hook's quietly voiced accusation.

'Oh, we will,' Hook said. He spoke a little more loudly now, and his voice was full of conviction. Lambert had noted years ago a capacity to sustain a role that came unexpectedly from this rubicund, slightly overweight figure. All coppers sometimes pretended to knowledge they did not have, but few of them were as convincing in producing bricks without straw as Bert Hook. Even Rushton believed for a moment that Hook had discovered some priceless piece of evidence that had escaped the rest of them. Bert was almost patronizing the men now as he explained himself. 'The Scene-of-Crime team have already sent several interesting items to Forensic. Science moves ahead of men like you two, fortunately.'

'You'll find nothing from us in that alley,' said the man opposite him. His denial did not carry the note of conviction, and Sturley flung a restraining hand on to his forearm.

Bert Hook studied the hand with interest, as if it were itself an admission. He noted that the man had known the location of Pegg's death, but did not trouble to follow up a point which would be readily denied. 'Every killer leaves something of himself behind at the scene of his crime.' Now he reached unhurriedly forward, ignoring Sturley's large hand, moving up to the point where the neck of the black T-shirt peeped out from beneath the leather waistcoat. He picked up a single hair between forefinger and thumb, held it speculatively against the light for an instant, then reached with his other hand into the pocket of his grey suit to produce a small polythene envelope. Three pairs of eyes followed his movements as he placed the hair within this container with infinite

71

care, then returned it whence it had come. The process seemed to give him much satisfaction.

He kept his eyes on the lesser man from whom he had gleaned the hair, not even bothering to watch the now more animated Sturley, as he addressed him. 'Nasty little graze, that, on your forehead, Mr Sturley. Bit too high for shaving, so you'll need to think of some other explanation. But it won't be any more convincing.'

Sturley's hand darted from his companion's arm to his own forehead, feeling the scab on the tiny scar as if he feared it was suddenly bleeding anew. 'I banged that in here, on the corner of a filing cabinet.' Ten minutes earlier, he would not even have offered an explanation. Now, it rang false and defensive, to him as well as to everyone else in that broad room. Every other sound had died with the piano at the end of the blowzy singer's ballad. It seemed as though all the ears of those lesser employees who had retired to the recesses of that dimly defined room were listening to his words and finding them unsatisfactory.

Hook shrugged, more elaborately than the men opposite him had shrugged at the outset of their exchanges. 'If you say so, Sturley. Forensic will tell us all about the smears of blood on the corpse which didn't come from Charlie. Just as they'll match up the hairs they found there with others, in due course. That's the beauty of science, you see; you can't argue with it.' He tapped the side pocket of his suit with satisfaction. 'I think we've got everything we need from here, sir. Unless of course you have further questions for these fools?' Only on the very last phrase did he allow the full depth of his disgust for the two vicious men in front of him to come through.

Rushton thought he had never seen a barren hand played so convincingly. He was experienced enough now not to risk overplaying it. 'Don't move out of the area without letting us know any new address,' he said. 'And give your position some thought. Consider just who it is you are protecting. He wouldn't hesitate to sacrifice you, and you know it.'

He knew that wouldn't work: they couldn't admit murder as they could a lesser crime and hope to mitigate it by implicating their employer. But it was the best he could manage by way of an exit line. He was very glad that he had brought Bert Hook with him. For a moment, he had even believed him about the blood on the corpse.

Bert Hook left without another word. He looked back from the exit at their adversaries, as if he was memorizing their every feature for future use. But it was the picture of Amy Pegg's grief-stricken face which filled his mind.

# 10

In another, more respectable part of the ancient city of Bristol, in the warm and well-lit offices on the fourth floor of a tower block, Detective Superintendent John Lambert was having his own problems.

He had spent another half hour with Pegg's little red book, then levered himself out of his swivel chair and set off in pursuit of James Berridge, who he was more than ever convinced was the force behind this murder. But the man was elusive. Even his personal secretary in the new office block did not know where he was. She was fifty, with well-coiffured grey hair and rimless glasses. She was efficient, experienced, and eminently respectable: just the kind of impeccable front that Berridge would have put in place here, Lambert reflected sourly.

And she was well versed in concealing her employer's whereabouts. When Lambert pressed, she referred him eventually to the only senior executive who was in the building, the head of his sales force. If someone was going to reveal the whereabouts of the boss to this persistent policeman, she knew her industrial procedures well enough to ensure that it would be someone who was paid to take the flak.

Lambert raised no objections to talking to Ian Faraday. He had found the initials 'I. F.' in Pegg's book, in a section which seemed to relate to James Berridge's flat in Old Mead Park. Berridge was a villain, though they had still to bring him to justice. Some of his enterprises were perfectly legal, a profitable and effective front for the darker activities which went on behind them and were the real source of his wealth. There was the same kind of mix among his employees; he had no idea yet into which category Ian Faraday might be placed.

The man was certainly nervous. His handshake had a practised firmness, but his limbs flailed a little wildly as he rearranged the two armchairs in front of his desk so that he could sit opposite his visitor. 'I'm afraid I'm not sure where Mr Berridge is today. Is it anything I might be able to help with?' he said rather breathlessly.

'Frankly, I don't know the answer to that. Do you have any connection with the Curvy Cats night club in Bristol?'

'No. Is the place a part of Mr Berridge's empire?' The denial came a little too quickly; the ignorance was protested insistently upon its heels.

'It is. Not a very pleasant one, to my mind. It calls itself a night club, but it's more a strip club, with extremely expensive entry fees and drinks.' And the kind of place where even more dubious and illegal arrangements were often completed.

Faraday nodded. 'It sounds like the club he has in London. I have nothing to do with that side of the group's activities. I am merely sales director for the clothing we make at our small factory in Stroud.'

Again he was firm about the disclaimer: Lambert found himself wondering about how his employer might have reacted to that. 'May I ask how many men you are responsible for?'

'Three. One of them is semi-retired now, but we keep him on for his contacts.' Not a big operation then; like the men's shops owned by Berridge in Oldford and Gloucester, this was no doubt a perfectly legal and modestly profitable business, a useful front behind which more evil dealings were conducted. Faraday had not hesitated over the information: he had the air of a man who seemed anxious to distance himself from Berridge's more nefarious activities, and from whatever major crime was the subject of the present enquiries. He seemed not at all surprised that a CID superintendent should be looking for his boss. And, Lambert now suspected, not at all anxious to protect him. This man might be a valuable contact if they were really going hard for his employer.

Lambert said, 'Have you ever heard mention of two men

called Jones and Sturley? They are based in the night club at Bristol. But we think they also have other functions.'

'No. I don't even know the names.'

'In that case, you should congratulate yourself. How long have you worked for the Berridge group?'

'Six years. I'm thirty-seven now.'

It was curious that he should volunteer his age like that. Lambert took it as a cue to assemble more personal details. 'Are you married?'

'No. Not any longer. I've been divorced for four years.' This time Lambert was amused rather than surprised by the detail. He found increasingly that heterosexuals wanted to assert that they were not gay. Even a failed marriage seemed to be taken as proof of that; people seemed unaware that on occasions it could indicate exactly the opposite.

As he sat in the armchair opposite his questioner, Faraday crossed his legs, but he was certainly not relaxed. His hands fluttered a little, and he had the air of a man constantly on the verge of revealing things about himself. That was a factor that was bound to interest detectives. He now said, 'Can you tell me what all this is about, Superintendent?'

Lambert smiled. 'I thought you might have asked that a little earlier. We are investigating the death of a man called Pegg, in Gloucester last night.'

Faraday pushed one of those too-mobile hands through a plentiful crop of dark-brown hair. 'I've never heard of him, I'm afraid. How did he die?'

'He was murdered, Mr Faraday. Expertly stabbed, with a knife which has not been recovered. He bled to death within a few minutes, but he was not found until this morning.'

Ian Faraday's brown eyes widened at the calm recitation of this detail. 'And – and you think that Berridge might be involved in some way in this?'

Lambert wondered whether the omission of any title for his employer signified anything. Hostility, he fancied: the man had at no point sought to defend his boss. 'We think Mr Berridge could help us with our enquiries. But we don't think he plunged a dagger into Charlie Pegg himself, and I'd rather you kept the subject of our investigation to yourself.

Now, bearing in mind the seriousness of this, can you give me any suggestion as to where your employer might be at this moment?'

'You've tried the London business number?'

'We've done more than that. We've sent people round there to look for him. He isn't either at the club or in his London flat. Nor is he at home in Oldford. We've tried his penthouse in Old Mead Park. He isn't there, and neither is his wife. Do you think he might be with her?'

Ian Faraday's clean-cut features were too expressive for his own good. They clouded, momentarily but significantly. 'No. I'm sure he isn't with Gabrielle.'

The use of the Christian name was surely noteworthy. He had not used Berridge's first name, and from what he had let slip about the man it seemed unlikely that there was much social interchange between them. As if he realized what he had done and was trying to retrieve it, Faraday said awkwardly, 'The Berridges don't go about much together nowadays. I believe they may – may even separate before too long. But perhaps I'm reading too much into things I've seen.'

Lambert thought of the initials in Charlie Pegg's book, and realized suddenly what the likely source of the small collection of words and initials he had listed under the number of the Berridges' penthouse apartment: an answerphone. If he was right, it meant this man had left messages on such a contraption. But by his own account, perhaps not for Berridge. He said, 'Do you visit them often at Old Mead Park?'

'No!' The vehemence seemed to take the speaker even more by surprise than his listener. Ian Faraday grinned sheepishly at it and said, 'I've been there, but I scarcely see Berridge at all outside this office. I've no desire to see him, as a matter of fact.' He opened his arms wide, then sat back on his chair and folded them, as if he felt that these recalcitrant limbs must be firmly controlled.

Lambert did not help him out; Faraday seemed to be in danger of stumbling into interesting revelations. The more he talked, the more this man seemed likely to be a valuable aid in any investigation into the more dubious activities of James Berridge. Faraday now waved those telltale hands in an unscripted arabesque, then clasped them firmly over his crossed right knee, as if his vocal cords lay there and might be stilled by his grasp. He smiled at his interrogator in a slightly embarrassed manner, but he managed to refrain from further words.

Lambert said brusquely, 'Let's leave your personal relationship with him for the moment.' He left the impression that he could unearth deeply compromising material at any moment he chose to do so. 'I've told you more than I should have about a brutal killing. I need to know where James Berridge is. I get the impression that some people round here have an idea where he might be. Frustrating the course of a police investigation can easily turn into a serious offence. I think you should tell me now where you think your employer may be; there will be no reason for me to tell him where the information came from, of course.'

The man opposite him had been looking increasingly confused and distressed. Berridge, as Lambert knew only too well, was not a man to cross. Faraday hesitated for a moment; then he was suddenly calm and determined, as if the decision he had taken had strengthened his resolution. 'You could try a woman called Sarah Farrell. I'm told she has a cottage on the outskirts of Gloucester. I don't know the number, but I expect she'll be in the book.'

'Thank you, Mr Faraday. I shan't tell Mr Berridge where the information came from. He will of course be able to find out easily enough that I have been talking to you. But you have done no more than your duty as a citizen. You should remind him of that if there is any unpleasantness.'

Lambert did not trouble to conceal the haste of his departure. He had wasted enough time locating James Berridge already. But he was also excited. Because the initials 'S. F.' had also figured in Charlie Pegg's cryptic little records.

Gabrielle Berridge found out the details of the death of poor Charlie Pegg without too much difficulty. George Lewis was very upset after the visit of the tall policeman to his little porter's office, and he was only too ready to talk about the death of his friend to the lady with the patrician manner and the sympathetic ear.

Gabrielle was surprised how much the death of Pegg affected Lewis: obviously the two had been closer than George had let on when he recommended Pegg for the work in her apartment. Well, that did not matter; the little man's work had been of a surprisingly high standard. She was sorry to see him go, especially like that. But she was not stricken with any great grief; she had scarcely known him, having been out of the flat for most of the days when he had worked there. She remembered how adamant James had been that he should not go into his study. Well, he would not need to worry about the busy little man any longer now.

And she herself would not be bothered by James for much longer. She shut out the fantasy of the life she would soon enjoy with Ian Faraday, for she had things to do now. As she went back into the penthouse, the phone was ringing, but she ignored it, as she had throughout the day. There was only one person whose calls she cared about, and she knew that he would not ring her here; not today. The rest of the calls could collect on the answerphone, to be answered later if she thought fit.

She went to the bottom drawer of her dressing table, removing the underclothes and stockings until she could slide her hand to the back and withdraw the small key she had hidden there. James would be furious if he knew she had it: the thought drew a small, secret smile to her lips.

She went through to his study, checking as she passed the picture windows of the drawing room that there was no sign of her husband's BMW in the drive or the car park. Then, with the infinite care of a safe-cracker, she slid the key into the lock of the top right-hand drawer of the big desk and eased it open. Even at this last moment of her treachery, apprehension held her still for a moment, during which she had time to notice the pounding of her heart and the trembling of her fingers.

But it was excitement, not fear, which eventually predominated. She took out the small black pistol and the box of ammunition, locked the drawer as carefully as she had opened it, and crept away to her bedroom to hide her booty.

Lambert looked up the address of Sarah Farrell in the phone book. But he did not ring before he visited her: it had been his aim throughout the day to confront James Berridge without any warning. He would have appreciated the solid presence of Bert Hook at his side, but to pick him up from the incident room in Oldford would have added another half hour to the journey, and there had been enough delays already.

Ms Farrell lived in the end one of a row of mews cottages, with a garage and a parking space discreetly tucked away behind it. It was a conversion of an old stable block which had been well done; the four cottages had a charm which far outstripped their humble origins. The front of the cottages faced north and there were three tall chestnuts shutting out the light at no great distance from them. This meant that the spring dark dropped early upon the lounges of these residences, for they were positioned beside the front doors with their brass lanterns. Two of the cottages already had lights on, but there was no light in the front room or the tiny hall of number four.

Lambert looked briefly to the rear of the cottage, and saw what he thought was Berridge's light-blue BMW there. That made him ring the bell insistently, even when at first there was no reply. Eventually, the little grille to the right of the door crackled into life, and an irritated female voice said, 'Well? Who is it?'

The sound made Lambert start, for he had not seen the grille. It seemed an unnecessary security refinement, in an area like this. He wondered if all the cottages had them. He stooped to the hidden microphone and said firmly, 'Police. We wish to speak to James Berridge.' Might as well let him think there was a full raiding party, if he was planning to be difficult.

There was a confusion of metallic murmurs before the distorted tones of Berridge came snarling through the device.

'I'm busy, Lambert. Why don't you piss off, instead of harassing innocent citizens?'

Lambert felt that being thus identified had lost him the first round in this strange contest. Had Berridge seen him arrive from behind the unlit windows? Or had he recognized his voice, even through that tinny medium? Perhaps he had been half-expecting him, though presumably not here. If so, it was further confirmation of a connection with Pegg's killing, though, like everything else they seemed to find out about James Berridge, quite useless in a court of law. Lambert rang the bell again lengthily and raised his voice from the discreet to the clamorous. 'Open the door, please. Unless you wish us to make the reason for this visit more public.'

A light went on suddenly behind the thick upstairs curtains, and there were muffled sounds of movement. A few moments later, the security locks on the door clicked back and it opened a reluctant six inches. Lambert moved forward immediately, like an importunate door-to-door salesman. 'Thank you. I need to see Mr Berridge urgently, or I should not have been so insistent.'

The woman looked at him for a moment with open hostility, then turned abruptly and went back into the lounge. She drew the curtains before she put on a light, so that for a moment they were in the inappropriate intimacy of darkness. When the standard lamp went on, she stood beside it, fastening the top button of her blouse before she looked at him. He stood awkwardly, a tall man whose head almost brushed the door frame of the small lounge, but she did not ask him to sit down.

She was quite small, though in this setting she did not appear so: she might have been chosen to complete the furnishings of that neat room with its Chinese carpet, its draped ruched curtains and its soft cream leather suite. There were no ceiling lights, so that it was impossible to speculate whether the blonde hair which gleamed lustrously in the light of the lamp was natural or contrived. She had clear skin and a well-formed figure; she checked the side fastening of her expensive skirt as if to draw attention to her slim waist. Her eyes glittered blue and angry as she faced him. 'You people have a bloody cheek! You barge in here without –'

'Sometimes it is necessary for us to be determined. Sometimes the people we wish to see can be very elusive.'

She whirled angrily away from him. In that small room, it was not possible for her to put much distance between them, but she busied herself pointedly with the things she might have done had she been alone. She switched on the small brass wall lights on each side of the fire, then lit the living-flame gas fire with a violent twist of its electronic starter.

Lambert was pleased to be ignored: he had no intention of getting involved in an argument with this woman. If she had thought to embarrass him by leaving him standing, she failed completely. He was well used to hostile receptions, and he had no wish to confront James Berridge from the comfortable depths of one of the armchairs. He stood quite still, listening intently to the sounds from the room above. He moved only when he heard the sound of feet on the stairs behind him. At that point, he stepped briskly into the centre of the room and turned to confront the man he had sought out here.

James Berridge was flushed and breathing heavily. He had scarcely troubled to disguise the fact that he had been in bed with the woman who had admitted Lambert. His tie was still unfastened, his hair a little tousled. The flush on his face no doubt came as much from the pleasures which had been interrupted as from the annoyance he felt at this untimely presence. Lambert was reminded of his first gaffer in London a quarter of a century earlier, who had believed in bursting in to catch villains between the blankets whenever possible. 'A man who's bollock-naked never feels in a position to argue,' had been his dictum. 'Take 'em on the nest and keep 'em away from their pants until the tarts are well into their knickers!' Those had been cruder days, with simpler criminals than this. Now he had unwittingly brought the old man's precepts into play with this subtler and greater villain. Well, there was no harm in that.

James Berridge was a powerful man, capitulating a little to the thin layer of fat which descends so easily upon affluence, but with the build and upper-body strength of a wrest-ler. He paused inside the door, setting himself in balance upon his powerful legs, as though he might spring at any moment upon this unwelcome visitor. He was very angry, but he was too practised in his dealings with the police to let anger take him over. Exasperation could upset the judge-ment, could lead a man into intemperate action. It was intensely annoying that this tiresome enemy should have tracked him here, but no more than that. His traces were well covered; this man could be no threat, if he kept his head. And he never had difficulty in doing that, nowadays.

He said, 'You've got a hell of a cheek! Who told you I was here?'

'We have our methods.' Lambert did not think it would take James Berridge long to find out who had given him the name of Sarah Farrell, but he would not help him. Perhaps Ian Faraday would have his excuses ready. 'We take a little trouble, when there is a serious crime involved.'

'If your methods were more efficient, you wouldn't waste time interrupting the lives of honest businessmen.' Berridge knew it was no more than the preliminary fencing, but he went through the ritual, as if he might lose face by not observing it, like some Japanese tycoon. He had not seen Lambert for over two years, since he had last shrugged off his accusations and got the better of him. He thought the man was looking older. There was a greater grizzling of grey amidst the plentiful crop of hair, and more lines around the grey eyes which studied him so steadily. Perhaps there was a hint of the tall man's stoop as he stood not more than five feet away. This evidence of frailty gave Berridge a sense of superiority.

Lambert said, 'A man who worked for you has been killed.'

'I'm not aware that any of my employees have not appeared today.' He liked the formality of that; it enabled him to mock without appearing to do so. He was aware of Sarah behind the superintendent, watching the exchange: it made him careful to be even calmer.

'A man called Charles Pegg. He worked in your flat at Old Mead Park. Doing work for you and your wife.' Lambert had his eyes fixed on the small patch of skin and chest hair he could see where Berridge had missed a button on the front of his shirt.

Berridge smiled, taking care not even to glance at Sarah Farrell. 'No doubt he was retained by Gabrielle to construct certain additions to the furnishings. I tend to leave these things to her.'

'Pegg knew quite a lot about you. Damaging things.'

'Which he no doubt failed to communicate to you, as you show no signs of producing them. And now he's dead. Look, Lambert, I've heard quite enough of your fairy tales before. If you've nothing better to offer me than this, then I suggest —'

'Where were you last night, Mr Berridge?'

'It's none of your business. But I'll indulge you, if it will get rid of you more quickly. I was in London. You can check it out easily enough.'

'I expect we shall. But I have no doubt you were where you say. You always did take care to be well out of the way when the dirty work went on.'

'It's a trick I learned from the police, I expect. What *is* your detection rate for burglaries in the last year, Lambert?'

'What was your business in London?'

Berridge had not expected this. He had been prepared to brazen out questioning about the mean little street where Pegg had been struck down, to enjoy baiting this flatfoot from the strength of a cast-iron alibi. He said, 'That's my affair. I have no intention of discussing my business concerns with you.'

Sarah Farrell said suddenly, 'I think I shall go and make some tea,' and moved towards the door into the kitchen.

Without detaching his eyes from Lambert, Berridge said, 'Don't do that. We'll get rid of this pig first. Then we can take the tea back to bed.' Through his mirthless smile, Lambert detected the first faint signs of worry. Like many careful planners, Berridge was disconcerted when events did not follow the course he had envisaged.

'They've arrested a man in London, you see. One of a chain of drug dealers. He's begun to talk about the people who employ him. About those who set up the big deals.

Some interesting names have come up. Not unexpected, but interesting.'

'And no doubt they include mine. They would, if you were involved.'

'Oh, you know I couldn't tell you that. Not at this stage.' Lambert had gone as far as he dared. It was a phone call from the drug squad that morning which had both given him information and authorized him to dangle this much in front of Berridge. There were men already under surveillance in Bristol whom Berridge would surely have to contact, if he was worried about his drug deals. If he did, they would be pulled in. And in view of what was now known about their activities, they would surely talk.

Berridge fell into a bravado he would not have attempted before he was rattled. 'Of course you won't tell me, because there is nothing to tell. You've made the mistake of making allegations in front of a third party this time.' For the first time since he had entered the room, he glanced at the blonde woman beyond his adversary, as if reassuring himself about her support. 'I'm sure my lawyers would be very interested to –'

'Your lawyers will soon be fully occupied with your defence, I think. In the meantime, I am concerned with a murder investigation. Will you tell me what orders you issued yesterday to two men called Jones and Sturley?'

'None at all. I give those men no orders. They are under the control of the manager of my club in Bristol.'

'Yes. It's surprising that you even recognize their names so promptly.'

Berridge's brain was racing, not with this, but with the suggestion that the police had information about his drug deals. 'I know nothing about the way Pegg died. I expect he had it coming to him, if he went about prying into the affairs of his betters and grassing on them.' There had been no suggestion until now that that was the reason for his death. It was an admission, a minor mistake, but again not one which would be worth anything in the hands of the Crown Prosecution Service.

Lambert said, 'Sturley and Jones will talk, once we have

them pinned down. They might even save themselves a few years in a high-security nick, once they reveal who gave them their orders to kill little Charlie Pegg.'

He turned for a moment to Sarah Farrell, whose blue eyes were open wide as they caught the light from the standard lamp. 'I'm sorry I had to come into your house like this. Perhaps you should be more careful of the company you keep.' He opened the door himself, then passed out through it without a further glance at the man he had come to see.

Berridge stared at the inside of the door for a full half minute, as if its dark wood could reveal the full extent of the knowledge possessed by his tormentor. The woman behind him said eventually, 'I'll get that tea now, and we'll go back upstairs, as you said. If you'd like to —'

'Forget it!' Berridge said harshly. 'Go into the kitchen and make us a snack. Put the radio on. And shut the door.'

She looked for a moment as though she might disobey him, her face whitening with fury. Then she snatched at the brass handle of the door and went out of the room, slamming it fiercely behind her.

When the music blared out from the transistor in the kitchen, Berridge reached for the phone. At least the instrument here would not be tapped. For the first time in years, he felt the stirrings of panic.

# 11

Christine Lambert watched her husband's head beginning to nod in front of the television set. Soon his chin would drop on to his chest and he would be well away. If he woke in less than half an hour, he would protest that he had never really been asleep, that he had merely taken refuge from 'this rubbish'. With that, his gesture towards the technicolour blinkings from the corner of the room would suggest that it was she who had introduced these banalities into their living space, whereas it was he who had switched on automatically before he slumped into his chair for the evening. John could be reassuringly male at times.

She had better strike before he subsided. 'You haven't forgotten that Caroline and the family are here for the weekend?' she said.

'Of course I haven't,' he said. It had merely slipped his mind: he hadn't really forgotten it. He stirred his defensive mechanisms into action. 'I may have to go to the golf club on Saturday, though. We've to play the next round in the knockout, and I think our opponents can only play then.'

Christine smiled, recognizing the tactical withdrawal she had often heard before. 'That won't be a problem. So long as you make sure to be your normal sunny self when you come back.'

'When did you know me any other way? I'll make polite conversation with my son-in-law; I'll wash up; I'll even read to the children. Probably *Winnie the Pooh* again, I expect. They seem to want to hear it over and over.' He tutted in deprecation, though secretly he looked forward to laughing conspiratorially over Eeyore and Piglet again with the youngsters on his knee. He had taken to grandfatherhood with unexpected delight, though he made the protests expected of him about a full and noisy house.

'You'll know it by heart soon,' agreed Christine. 'But you'll survive. I expect you may even need to play golf on Sunday morning, if the going gets rough.' He grunted, apparently suddenly interested in the television programme he had just despised: there was no point in acknowledging how thoroughly she understood and indulged him nowadays.

She knew he was on a murder case, that she could prod him into talking a little about it, if she chose. The days when he had hugged the job to himself, had used his home as no more than a sleeping place, an unwelcome interruption to the intensity of his hunting of men, were long gone now. She found it difficult sometimes to understand how near she had come to leaving him, to taking her small daughters and herself to somewhere, anywhere, away from the mysteries of police work and its exclusive camaraderie of thief-takers.

Nowadays, she accepted that he would work fourteen-hour days when the job demanded it of him. She saw the adrenaline rise in him when the quarry was near, and found herself glad to see such energy and intensity still. But because she accepted these things, she was the more jealous of his leisure; she guarded his periods of regeneration away from the job, watching them as carefully as if she was protecting an invalid, instead of a man whose work-rate sometimes left younger CID officers protesting in his wake.

On that evening, he dozed a little longer in front of the television set. But at three in the morning, he was wide awake. She lay wordless beside his long body, aware without a word from him that he must feel himself close to an important arrest.

Policemen like to pretend to outsiders that they exist in a world of routine, where there are occasional dangers but few real excitements. It is a myth, of course; in part a reaction to the image of police work which the public has assembled for itself from the distortions of cinema and television over the years.

On that Thursday morning in Oldford, the CID room was more animated than Bert Hook could ever remember seeing it. He was reminded of those scenes in the war films of his youth, in which information poured into a tense operations room and the picture of triumph or disaster gradually emerged over the hours. Normally, police work produced results over weeks, even months, of painstaking routine. Just occasionally, as this morning, the results of that work came together, the different strands began to interweave, and the pace quickened towards a result.

Every few minutes, there seemed to be some new small item which built towards the outcome they all wanted, so that the cumulative effect of the efforts of different sectors gave an air of inevitability to the downfall of James Berridge. There was a phone call from Forensic about some fibres of cotton found on the body of Charlie Pegg, a sighting of William Sturley in the Star and Garter in the hours before Pegg's murder, news from the drug squad of a most interesting meeting later in the day between two of the barons of that evil industry.

Everything suggested that they would be able to arrest James Berridge before the day was over.

To understand the excitement in the CID section, one would have had to have been a party to the unsuccessful attempts to bag Berridge over the preceding years. Most of the men who gathered round Rushton's computer screen on that morning had been involved. Two years ago, they had almost had him. Then a key witness had refused to testify, and two others had disappeared. Berridge had enjoyed their frustration. And none of those involved had forgotten that enjoyment.

By eleven o'clock there was enough information to bring in William Sturley and Walter Jones for further questioning about the murder of Charlie Pegg; Rushton began setting up an identity parade for Sturley. The two hard men were picked up as they arrived at the Curvy Cats. By midday, Lambert was equipped with search warrants for the business and domestic premises of James Albert Berridge.

There was one snag. No one knew exactly where Berridge

was. The grey-haired personal assistant at the Bristol offices was today more directly helpful: Berridge had been expected at the office, but had not arrived. That was unusual, but what was without precedent, she insisted, was that he had not phoned in to announce any change of plans. Like many major crooks, Berridge was punctilious about the etiquette of regular business practice.

He was not at the Bristol club. The anxious voice of the manager of the Curvy Cats, John Murray, assured them of that. He was not in London. There was no reply from his home number in Old Mead Park. Nor, on this occasion, was there any reply from the mews cottage on the outskirts of Gloucester which Sarah Farrell had so grudgingly allowed John Lambert to enter nineteen hours earlier.

There was muttered speculation among those on the fringe of the hunt that the bird had flown. Two of the younger detective constables were nodding to each other and exchanging defeatist whispers about Marbella and the Costa Crime when Rushton descended angrily upon their inexperience. They had not known until now that the detective inspector's invective could be so inventive and colourful, nor that his passion could run so high when the morale of his team was at stake. 'In any case,' he concluded his tirade, 'you should be aware that for drugs offences we would get him back, even from Spain. Of course, you might have a limited interest in that, if you were back on the beat by then.'

Lambert chafed at this last delay when he was so close to his prey. Eventually, he left Rushton with instructions to contact him on the car phone with news of any developments and took Hook out with him to the old Vauxhall. He did not understand this: if Berridge had moved far from home, he should have been picked up.

It was quiet in the middle of the day as they drove up the wide black tarmac drive of Old Mead Park. In the trimly kept communal gardens of the residences, pink and red camellias were still in full flower, and the bright blaze of the first Japanese azaleas lit up the front of the beds as the sun was hazed by high clouds. The birds sang of burgeoning spring and the gardens of diligent horticultural effort, but there was no visible human presence on the wide green lawns. High above them, as they got out of the old car in the deserted car park, the wide spans of the double glazing of the penthouse flat gleamed out over the landscape. It was impossible to tell from below whether any unseen observer had noted their arrival.

The place was eerily quiet. It was almost a relief when George Lewis came out from his porter's office to meet them. 'Good morning, Superintendent Lambert,' he said. Not many people recalled a detective's name after a single meeting. Lambert reflected that a memory for names was probably a useful part of Lewis's working equipment.

At least he could reciprocate. 'Have you seen Mr Berridge go out this morning, George?' He made no reference to their conversation about Berridge on the previous day, sensing that Lewis would be a little flattered if he thought it was a secret between them.

The porter shook his head. 'Haven't seen anyone from the penthouse today. He usually goes out early, if he's here. Of course, I don't see all the comings and goings. I have other duties as well.' But his slight smile indicated that he was confident he saw most of the daylight activity. Certainly, the square window of his office commanded a comprehensive view of the drive which all must use for arrivals and departures, as well as a side view of many of the garage doors which were discreetly screened by rows of shrubs in the basement storey of the exclusive block.

Lambert said, 'We need to get into the penthouse flat. There is no need for you to alarm the rest of the residents with this, George, though the news will get round quickly enough. We are here to arrest James Berridge.'

Lewis's reaction amused Bert Hook. It was that of the trained butler rather than the porter. His eyes opened a little wider, but his features remained otherwise impassive, as if it was a professional challenge not to register shock or emotion. He did not say, 'Indeed, sir,' as Hook half-expected from the rest of his bearing. Instead, he turned quietly and unlocked the steel cupboard behind him which resembled a small safe. 'You won't mind if I accompany you into the flat, gentlemen?' he said, producing a bright metal key. 'The Residents' Committee would prefer it, I think.' His bearing announced that if there was to be any melodrama, it would be even more important that the etiquette of the occasion was properly observed. George Lewis put on his smart green porter's jacket and straightened the knot of his tie.

'It's very quiet round here today,' said Hook as they went up in the near-silent lift. He wasn't sure himself whether he was merely making conversation or gathering information against all eventualities, as was the normal CID officer's instinct.

Lewis seemed to have caught the same need for precision. 'There are usually only four of the eleven residences occupied in the middle part of the day,' he said with authority, as they moved over a carpeted landing to the door of the penthouse. 'And sometimes it is fewer than that, if the occupants are out shopping.'

They heard the electric bell ringing clearly inside the apartment; as they had expected, there was no sign of movement in response. At a nod from Lambert, the porter inserted the skeleton key and the lock turned smoothly. 'It's the first time I've been in here since I came to let in Charlie Pegg and set him to work for Mrs Berridge,' he said, as he turned the brass handle and pushed on the rosewood panel. Probably he spoke just for the sake of words, trying to disperse the tension they all felt suddenly rising as the door opened and the oblong of light fell upon the landing. But the mention of his murdered friend seemed only to add to it.

Lambert moved swiftly through the huge drawing room, with its panoramic views over the Gloucestershire countryside, into the dining room, with its oval mahogany table and reproduction Chippendale chairs. The kitchen was neat, almost clinical in its cleanliness; there was no crockery in the washing-up machine. The arrays of units were surely far too elaborate for the culinary requirements of the two residents. After a moment's hesitation, he pushed open the door of the main bedroom, noting in passing the two pillows at the middle of the top of the king-sized bed, indicating perhaps that one person slept alone on that generous surface.

The *en suite* bathroom was empty. So were the main bath-room and the second bedroom.

Hook, feeling like a character on stage, went and opened the door of a cloaks cupboard near the entrance. He saw only three coats and a vacuum cleaner; no body tumbled hideously forward into the room. He rejoined the others in what was plainly James Berridge's study. It was as deserted as the rest of the penthouse. Lambert walked over to the desk and tried the top right-hand drawer; rather to his surprise, it was not locked. But it was empty apart from some blank envelopes and writing paper. The other drawers of the desk were locked. He resisted the impulse to investigate further, to open cabinets and look for evidence which might help to put Berridge away. There would be time for that in due course. Better to let the fingerprint boys loose before they began to open desks and filing cabinets.

He said to Lewis, 'When was Berridge last here, George?'

The porter shook his head reluctantly, as though to confess ignorance was a blot on his professional expertise. 'I couldn't say. I haven't seen him for a couple of days. But I finish officially at six in the evenings and I can't see as much from my flat as from the office. In any case, I have very little idea of who is coming and going in the hours of darkness. The Berridges have two garages, but they are on the other side of the block from my place, so I don't hear any sounds of activity from there.'

'We'd better check those garages before we go.'

Lewis nodded and began the business of closing doors and locking up the apartment. It took a little time to descend to the garages beneath the block; during this interval, Hook and Lambert elicited the information that the Berridges rarely moved about together, that they seemed more and more to lead independent lives. Lambert thought merely that it was a mercy that Mrs Berridge was not likely to be too devastated when her husband was put away for a long stretch. In view of what they found in the next few minutes, the information suddenly became of much greater interest.

Lewis said, 'Most of the owners have electronic controls for these garage doors, but I can override them. I have to be able to open them by hand, for safety reasons, you see.' It was another small assertion of his importance in his official function; Hook and Lambert exchanged smiles behind his back as he bent to the lock. He fiddled for a moment with the small, flat key, then slid up the door of Gabrielle Berridge's garage. It was empty; the tiny patch of fresh oil from the engine sump was all that the daylight revealed in that bare concrete box.

When the panting Lewis eased up the door of the adjoining garage, there was more material for them. James Berridge's light-blue BMW gleamed smooth and bright, as if welcoming the light as an opportunity to show off its contours. They were looking at the passenger side of the vehicle, and at first they thought it was empty. Then, as they moved round behind the boot and saw that the driver's door was open, they realized that it was not.

James Berridge's body lay half in and half out of the vehicle, with the head twisted at an odd angle against the concrete floor. The single eye which remained was open, frozen in a permanent expression of surprise. Most of the back of the head was shot away; the pistol must have been pressed against the temple. A long smear of grey and crimson matter was mercifully shadowed by the body of the car.

The pistol lay where it had apparently fallen, beneath James Berridge's twisted right wrist.

# 12

The Scene-of-Crime team was as diligent in its attention to the area around the body of James Berridge as it would have been in investigating the death of any more admirable citizen. George Lewis was impressed as he watched the comings and goings of the officers and glimpsed what little he could of their work in the garage.

Once they had their tapes erected to seal off the area of the search, they brought in extra lighting, directing their arc lamps under the vehicle they could not move until they had examined the ground beneath it in minute detail. Lewis was delighted to discover a role for himself. By acting as an unofficial barrier between the busy policemen and the curious residents who paid his salary, he could find out most of what was going on.

He made tea and biscuits for the Scene-of-Crime team, then fed snippets of what he had learned to the curious residents of Old Mead Park about the sensational event in the basement. Passing to and fro outside the garage as the day progressed, George saw what he presumed was human hair, strands of various fibres, even what looked like minute samples of grime and oil, being carefully labelled in their polythene envelopes for dispatch to the forensic laboratories. Retailing some of this to the residents as they passed his room, the porter watched with satisfaction as those respectable eyes widened.

The fingerprint officer, his feet covered like those of his colleagues in plastic bags to protect whatever evidence lay beneath his tread, dusted every surface that seemed remotely hopeful with his mysterious powder, systematically treating both the exterior and the interior of the BMW before he moved on to the garage doors and the plastic light and power switches. Then he steeled himself to give the same treatment to the corpse itself and the pistol that had almost certainly been the instrument of his death. His last task before he left was to press the fingers of the dead man on to a prepared surface, so that he would have clear prints for elimination purposes.

It was three hours before Lambert and Hook returned. They watched impassively as the mortal remains of James Albert Berridge were put into the death wagon. Lewis, appearing silently at their heels, said, 'Away to the funeral parlour at last, is he, Mr Lambert?' The residents would want all the gory details; for a day or two at least, and perhaps for longer if he used this affair skilfully, the porter would be a little more than the reassuring but anonymous presence which he normally was for most of them. Information increased a man's standing and interest. Lewis, erect if a trifle portly in his official uniform, presented himself to the man in charge of the case as the intelligence officer for the residents of Old Mead Park.

The superintendent understood that Lewis's standing might be increased by information, and was prepared to offer a little, knowing that he needed to question the porter in due course. 'I'm afraid it may be some time before he reaches the funeral parlour, George. There'll be a postmortem first, and then an inquest.'

Lewis nodded, putting his hands for a moment in the jacket pockets of his uniform, trying to appear insouciant in the face of death, as the van reversed carefully away from the garages with its grisly burden. 'Will they try to find out why he killed himself at the inquest?'

'Not exactly that. The main purpose of an inquest will be to establish exactly what kind of death this was. Whether it really was suicide, for instance, George.'

The porter's eyes widened. Noticing one of the residents regarding him curiously from a distance, he took his hands out of his pockets and fastened the top button of his green jacket, though the afternoon sun was now at its warmest.

'You think someone waited in there and shot him?' He gestured with his head towards the dark cavern of the garage, where Sergeant Johnson and his SOC team were concluding their work.

'I'm trying not to think anything until I have more facts, George. We don't even know when he died yet, but we should have an idea about that by the end of the day. Do you recall seeing any strangers about the place, last night or this morning?'

George frowned, making sure he gave the question the attention it deserved. He would have liked to be able to put forward a sinister, armed figure, but that was clearly not on. 'No, I didn't. I told you, I'm off duty between six p.m. and nine a.m., and my flat is on the other side of the building from these garages.' He brightened a little. 'The milkman is usually here by seven-thirty, and the postman comes about eight. You could ask them.'

'That's already in hand. Is there a paperboy?'

'No. The milkman brings in the papers, Monday to Saturday.'

Lambert nodded. 'We shall be asking your residents if they saw anyone, in due course. This may turn out to be a murder enquiry, George.'

'Surely not.' It was impossible to say whether this was a conventional expression of horror at the darkest crime of all or a genuine view. As if seeking to explain himself, Lewis stumbled on. 'I mean, I know he had plenty of enemies –'

'How do you know that, George?' It was Bert Hook, whose presence the porter had almost forgotten, who had interrupted. Lewis was startled for a moment by the challenge. 'Well, I've heard the odd story. And Charlie Pegg told me to watch out for him, when I got the job here. And I've seen him once or twice at nights, with men who looked like minders to me.'

Lambert said quietly, 'I told George that Berridge was a villain, Bert, before all this happened. When we were still looking into Charlie Pegg's death.'

'I guessed it for myself anyway. I've kept my eye on him for two years, after what Charlie told me when I got the job here.' Having asserted this, the porter was silent for a moment. Perhaps the time when they had searched the rooms of the penthouse before discovering the grim scene in the garage seemed already much more than four hours earlier, as it did to them. 'He killed Charlie Pegg, didn't he? For grassing on him.'

Lambert glanced at him sharply, wondering for a moment if he knew more than he had admitted to about Pegg's activities within this block. It did not seem very likely: Pegg had been a loner, careful with his knowledge, like most snouts who lasted any length of time. He remembered Lewis's account of how Pegg had saved his life in their National Service days, and thought that such closeness should allow a man a little knowledge about the death of his friend.

He said quietly, 'Yes, George. He didn't strike Charlie down, but he killed him just as much as if he'd handled the knife himself. The men who did it were his men, acting on his orders. You'll be glad to know that we have them in custody. And thanks to our Forensic people, we can prove they killed Charlie. We came here this morning to arrest Berridge on the grounds of that and other very serious charges.'

George Lewis looked with silent satisfaction at the now locked and empty garage. 'If he killed Charlie Pegg, I'm glad someone got here before you did.' On this ruthless statement, he turned away, as if he acknowledged now that the drama was ended and he must get on with the other, more mundane, tasks that he had postponed to attend upon it. He moved without grace, a short, tubby figure in his rather ridiculous uniform. But his sturdy loyalty to the dead friend who had moved from jailbird to craftsman and police informer gave him an undeniable dignity.

The CID men followed him into his office, where he was able to give them a surprising amount of detail about the daily activities of the residents of Old Mead Park. Hook noted the details in his rapid, round hand: his notes would be a useful check against the more detailed door-to-door interviews which were already being launched above and around them by the junior officers of the team.

George Lewis's most interesting piece of information was

a negative one. It seemed that Mrs Berridge had been at Old Mead Park in the earlier part of the previous day. But he had not seen or heard anything of her since then.

Sarah Farrell rang in to the travel shop at four o'clock. 'I shall be back in tomorrow. Have there been any problems?'

'Nothing we couldn't cope with. We're perfectly OK, you know. There's no need for you to rush back until you're feeling completely well.' There was no necessity to let the manager think she was indispensable. In the travel agent's office, the older woman who answered her call tried to fill her tones with concern, but she was more worried about asserting her own competence.

Sarah understood that. She did not resent it; she was pre-occupied in any case with more important personal consider-ations. 'That's all right. I know you can cope, but I'll be better at work.' For a moment, she had forgotten what excuse she had given for her absence. She remembered now, just in time: it was an imagined illness her mother had suffered. 'Mum's getting better now, anyway. They thought it might be pneumonia, but it was only a chill. Thank heavens for antibiotics! I should be in tomorrow at the usual time. Thanks for holding the fort. Did the new winter brochures come in from Thomson's?'

One thing about all that was true, Sarah thought as she put the phone down. She would be better at work than on her own with her memories in the little mews cottage.

She went automatically to switch on the radio, as she nor-mally did when she was working alone in the cottage. Then she thought better of it. The news of the death of James Berridge had been relayed in the bulletin at one o'clock, and there would probably be no addition to what had been announced then. She knew all that she needed to know about the death of the man who had been her lover.

She looked again at the great stain on the lounge wall-paper. She would have a go at cleaning it up, once she felt up to it. They said red wine was the worst of all to shift: she might have to redecorate. Then she wandered through into the cloakroom and studied the livid bruising around her closed right eye in the antique oval mirror over the small washbasin. She would need a story for that when she went in tomorrow: even the most skilful make-up would not cover that from the sharp eyes of her staff. Fair skin was always the worst for showing up such damage.

Her head still ached, but she was too restless to sit still. When she tried to read a book, the print danced before her eyes and her mind strayed obstinately elsewhere. She had a feeling that there was something she had omitted, some obvious step that she had overlooked in her distress. When she went upstairs and looked in the black leather handbag she used most often, she realized what it was.

There followed an absurd half hour of black comedy when she tried to dispose of the things. She looked automatically at the empty fireplace, but she knew immediately that the solution was not there. She rarely lit a fire, for the central heating kept the small house as warm as anyone could wish it; in any case, the things would never be properly destroyed by the heat she could muster from her living-flame gas fire.

She dropped them into the wastebin beneath the kitchen sink, then hastily retrieved them. She had heard of them examining people's rubbish. If the sociologists found out all kinds of interesting things about people that way, the police would surely not neglect it. She thought about the recesses of the rubbish bag in the dustbin outside, but it would be four days yet before it was collected, so that was no good. She almost dropped the things into the waste disposal unit. Then, at the last moment, she wondered if they might break the machine; she had never fed anything into it but kitchen waste. If the things broke it, that would draw attention to the very secret she was trying to conceal.

Eventually she went out to the garden behind the cottage, looking right and left like a thief to check that she was not observed. There was no one in sight. She had better be quick: there was no knowing when the long arm of the law would appear. She smiled bleakly when that phrase came so automatically to mind: it was the way her father had always described the police, in those far-off days when to his small daughter they had seemed a remote but friendly force.

She was no gardener. Her status as professional woman had demanded that she paid the pensioner in the cottage opposite hers to tend her small, neat plot. But she managed to find a trowel in the corner of the garage. Then she almost made an elementary mistake. The first hole she dug was amongst the wallflowers which had opened their brilliant palette in the bed beneath her kitchen window in the last week. Just in time, she realized that these plants would be removed before long, and the ground forked over for the summer bedding. What she was burying might be turned up before the curious old eyes of her gardener.

She moved unsteadily across the tiny lawn in her inappropriate high heels and selected a place among the shrubs which screened the rear of the property. It did not take long to make a small hole, even in that clay soil. It was only about eight inches deep, but that would be enough. She took a last look at the car keys, then dropped them neatly at the bottom of the hole.

They disappeared quickly as the loose soil tumbled back over them. It was almost as if the small white hands which manipulated the trowel belonged to some other, anonymous female. She slid the sole of her unsuitable shoe lightly back and forth over the surface, as if confirming to herself that the deed was done, and went swiftly back into the garage with her trowel. She thought she caught a movement behind the curtains to her right, and had a moment of panic. Then her feeling of relief returned: if any curious eyes had indeed watched her, they could surely not have realized what she was about.

Once she was back in the house, she felt more at ease. And with that relaxation, energy returned to her. She emptied the books from the glass-fronted bookcase, then tugged it three feet along the wall until it covered the stain of the wine. That would have to do, until she could get down to some more permanent repair. When she had shifted the two armchairs and moved the standard lamp into the corner where the bookcase had been, the arrangement did not look too contrived. She restored the books to their shelves and made

101

herself a hot drink before she subsided rather breathlessly into her armchair. The exercise had been good for her, she decided, as she sipped her tea and studied the results.

She wondered when the police would arrive.

# 13

Cyril Burgess, M.B., Ch.B., was working late. Policemen are accustomed to pursue crime outside office hours, but Burgess was a civilian. He had agreed to speed the investigation into the death of James Berridge by conducting his autopsy as immediately as other pressing work allowed.

It was now eight o'clock on this early spring evening, and he was feeling virtuous. He was also pleased with his findings, and prepared to exhibit his pleasure to his old friend and sparring partner, John Lambert. He peeled off his polythene gloves and said, 'Set up to look like a suicide, John. But not one, in my opinion. I'll do you a written report tomorrow, when my scribe returns to duty, but I can tell you the essentials now.'

Lambert thought how different Burgess looked now from the man he saw in his office, where his Savile Row suits and immaculate shirts made even much more dapper plain-clothes men than himself feel shabby. The pathologist looked larger and heavier now, in his green overalls and short green Wellington boots. The loose jacket made his arms seem massive; the rather ridiculous green denim hat completed the effect which made him seem more like a butcher than the doctor he had once been. That is what he was in essence, thought Lambert: a butcher, but with a scientific interest in the processes of dismemberment and analysis. He said, 'If it isn't suicide, that won't be altogether a surprise. He was a thoroughgoing villain whom we were about to arrest on drugs charges. We should probably have charged him with murder as well, in due course. But what makes you so certain this wasn't suicide?'

Burgess swept the sheet from the top of the corpse with the casual expertise of a stage magician. Lambert flinched a little, but his reaction disappointed Burgess, who had hoped to derive a little innocent fun from the squeamish stomach of the superintendent. Lambert had been prepared for this, and the fact that he had seen the gory scene in the garage made the remains of the head less shocking. The pathologist said, 'The weapon was held against the left temple of the deceased: as the bullet blew most of that side of the head away, you'll have to take my word for that. But you can see at least one edge of the cavity where it emerged. Incidentally, there was blood all over the interior of the car, as you probably saw. Whoever shot him must have had blood on his clothes. But I expect he'll have disposed of those, now that he's had twenty-four hours to himself. Or herself, of course.' Burgess appeared to find these reflections quite satisfying.

He turned to what remained of the skull; Lambert found it disturbing that it was obviously so light, so that it moved like the head of a ventriloquist's dummy. The blackened flesh of the lower half of the face grinned an awful grin at him, like an eroded gargoyle. He said, 'Yes. We found the bullet in the wall on that side of the garage. And the man wasn't left-handed.'

Burgess was disconcerted. It looked as though the detection team had already come to the conclusions he thought so clever in himself. He said, 'Almost certainly a right-handed man committing suicide would have shot himself in the right temple. Incidentally, scarcely anyone shoots himself in a car. The pipe from the exhaust is the popular method, and with good reason. It is reasonably painless and one sinks into oblivion without leaving a mess like this for others to discover and clear up.' He gestured towards the various human items he had chosen to investigate, all of them at present decently hidden under covers on the surface next to the stainless-steel sink where water still ran, slowly and silently washing away the human detritus deriving from his efforts.

Lambert said, 'You saw where the body lay?'

'Yes. With only the feet still in the car. I asked the SOCO's team not to move the body until the photographer had shots of it from three different angles.' Burgess loved not only the diversion of an 'interesting' death but the processes of detection. If he could involve himself in those, that would be his idea of a perfect professional day.

Lambert was prepared to indulge him. He knew that a pathologist who was anxious to help, who did not think merely in terms of providing safe legal testimony about a suspicious death, was a valuable aide. 'You thought the position of the body significant?'

Burgess paused, savouring the moment when his expertise was at the centre of an investigation. 'What was the weapon involved?'

'A Smith and Wesson .357 magnum handgun.' Which would no doubt be 'Exhibit A' in due course. 'Forensic should have the report on it available in the morning.'

'Right. So let me tell you what I think happened. In court, I should have to say that "the injuries were commensurate with . . ." or some other convenient circumlocution, but I'm telling you now that this is what I think happened. Someone was waiting in the car for your Mr Berridge. Probably he or she was crouching in the well behind the front seats; probably the victim never saw him. He pressed the revolver against the side of Berridge's head and fired. He was at a slight angle – the shot would have blown the whole of the head away otherwise. As it was, the impact was sufficiently violent to lift the corpse sideways, out of the car and into the position in which it was eventually discovered.'

Lambert nodded. 'Someone could also have got into the car with him – someone he thought was of no danger to him. If he wasn't expecting to be attacked, the element of surprise could be just as great.'

'I suppose so.' As Lambert had intended, Burgess was a little deflated; he had seen the event so vividly in his imagination that he had permitted himself no alternatives.

'Anything else about the death wound?'

'Only that a silencer certainly wasn't used. That single report must have been pretty deafening. Didn't anyone hear it?'

'No one that the door-to-door enquiries have flushed out

so far. That garage is in effect a concrete box in the basement. The noise in the immediate area would be deafening, but it would be contained. The garages have a thick concrete ceiling and the communal entrance hall is immediately above that particular section.'

'Isn't there a porter?'

'Not a twenty-four-hour one: the number of units in the block doesn't justify it, even though they're luxury flats. The porter lives on the site, but his flat's at the other side of the building. He certainly wouldn't have heard the noise from there if he was off duty.' What Burgess had given him so far did little more than confirm what the police team had decided before the body was brought here, but the pathologist's official view had its own value in days when any independent police opinion seemed to be open to challenge. It was time to get at the information which would pinpoint their questioning. 'What about time of death?'

'An impact such as this cadaver has suffered completely destroys the nervous system. That makes some of our tests difficult. But some of the old things are still useful. Stomach contents, for example.' Burgess slipped off his absurd hat, revealing the immaculate parting in his plentiful silver hair, and moved towards one of the smaller trays on the surface beside the sink. 'Would you like me to . . . ?'

'No, thank you. No demonstrations; just your findings, please.'

Burgess mimed his disappointment, though he had always known that Lambert would prevent him revealing what lay hidden. He wrinkled his nose a little, implying that he preferred the smell of decaying human remains to the all-pervading formaldehyde, which was after all a poison. 'Very well. Your man consumed a meal which looks to me like lasagne, with a custard tart and about half a bottle of wine. It was probably eaten four to five hours before he died.'

'Which was when?'

Burgess paused, enjoying the situation. 'Last night rather than this morning. Probably between ten p.m. and two a.m. – I wouldn't like to be more precise than that. If you could

106

find out exactly when he ate, I could probably be a little more definite.'

And whom he ate with, thought Lambert. He wondered how many people had seen Berridge alive after he had left Sarah Farrell; that period had just been dramatically narrowed. Had someone been waiting for Berridge's return to Old Mead Park? None of the residents had so far admitted to seeing or hearing anything suspicious. The time of death might explain why no one had heard the shot. If it had been before midnight, there would have been televisions or radios on in most of the flats which were occupied.

He said absently to Burgess, 'Thank you for your help, Cyril. I'll keep you informed of developments. This isn't the usual tragedy. I suppose someone will mourn for Berridge, but I for one won't be shedding any tears. He was a thorough-going ruffian: God knows how much misery and horror he's brought into other lives through the drugs he's supplied.'

'But he has the same right to have his murder investigated as any other citizen. The police can't discriminate about the way they uphold the law. Some superintendent told me that, only a couple of days ago.' It was so nearly what Lambert had emphasized at the time of Charlie Pegg's death that it was almost an echo. Cyril Burgess must have been aware of that, for he looked quite insufferably smug.

Lambert sighed. For the first time, he realized what a long day it had been. 'You're right, of course. Sometimes you want to set yourself up as judge and jury, but that way disaster lies. I warn young coppers about the danger often enough.'

They went out together into the darkness. The mortuary car park was deserted apart from Burgess's Jaguar and Lambert's old Vauxhall. They were on the edge of Oldford here, far from any streetlighting. The heavens were perfectly clear, so that remote planets were visible against the navy sky. Burgess mused:

> '. . . fairer than the evening air,
> Clad in the beauty of a thousand stars.'

Satisfied that death had been decently dressed with a quotation, he climbed into the Jaguar and drove off.

Lambert contemplated that vast and lonely silence for a moment, knowing that the intelligent and cultivated man who had just driven away felt as insignificant as he did beneath that sky. There was no sound, until the distant bleating of a tardy lamb brought him gently back to this earth.

He could not place the words Burgess had quoted. He tried to dismiss them and concentrate on the case as he drove home through the Gloucestershire lanes. When Burgess confirmed his findings in his report, it should make the 'Murder' verdict at the inquest straightforward. It would probably have to be accompanied by the standard 'By person or persons unknown', but a swift confession was still a possibility.

Perhaps the morrow would bring him the energy he had found so elusive so far. John Lambert could remember no murder hunt which had aroused less enthusiasm in him than that for the killer of James Albert Berridge.

He was almost home when the source of Burgess's quotation came belatedly to him; by that time he had ceased to puzzle over it. It was Marlowe's Helen, that starting point for so much disaster, who was 'fairer than the evening air'. Perhaps it would be the women in the case who would throw some light on this death.

He wondered why it had taken them most of the day to locate the wife of James Berridge.

# 14

Gabrielle Berridge was interviewed by Lambert and Hook at ten-thirty the next morning at Old Mead Park.

Less than an hour before this time, she had identified that shattered head at the mortuary as belonging to her late spouse, James Albert Berridge. They had been prepared for extreme distress at the grisly sight. But the widow had apparently found the experience less disturbing than might have been expected. She had driven her own car to the mortuary, composed herself in five minutes alone after the identification, and refused the offer of a lift home in a police car.

When she opened the door of the penthouse to admit them, the smell of percolating coffee drifted through from the kitchen behind her and she smiled at them as if they were welcome visitors, rather than outsiders intruding upon the intimacies of a widow's grief. It was almost as though she had the apartment up for sale and was greeting prospective purchasers. The officers had so wide an experience of bereavement and its effects that nothing could now shock them. But they found Gabrielle Berridge's reaction to this death interesting.

Lambert began with an apology for his team's searching of the rooms around them on the previous day. 'We made every effort to contact you before we entered.' He paused, but she busied herself with the tray and the coffee, offering neither resentment nor an explanation of her absence. 'It's our immediate routine, you see, in the case of a violent death. To take the commonest instance, there may be indications in the home of the deceased as to the reason for a suicide.'

She nodded her dark head, motioning them towards the

armchairs of the big three-piece suite in the sitting room. 'A note, you mean. And did you find such a note here?'

'No. Does that surprise you?'

She fastened her dark eyes upon his face, looking for clues about his thoughts, as if she, not he, was conducting this exchange and seeking for information. 'Nothing about James surprises me any more, Superintendent. I suppose I should now say "surprised".' For no more than an instant, her features brightened, as if the thought that her husband was now in the past gave her pleasure.

Lambert, deciding already that he need not tread too carefully through this woman's grief, studied those features for a moment before he spoke, but the mask had dropped back again. Beneath the ink-black hair, falling a little over her right eye as she turned to pour the coffee, her face was pale but composed. There was no sign of the puffing around the eyes which would denote that tears had been shed before their arrival. As she handed him the delicate china cup, her hand shook a little, but she looked excited rather than grief-stricken. She said, 'So when did James kill himself, Mr Lambert?'

Lambert was here to study her, as well as to acquire information, and he did so coolly, almost insultingly, now. Spouses were always the prime suspects in domestic murders, and this one had absented herself mysteriously in the hours after the death. 'This was not suicide, Mrs Berridge. There is no reason why you should not know that; I am already quite sure that the Coroner's Court will return a verdict of "Murder".' Not, in fact, as sure as he pretended, for that would involve a jury, and juries, like committees, are unpredictable devices. An 'Open' verdict was still possible, unless he could produce more evidence than the forensic findings on the way that pistol had been used.

Gabrielle Berridge raised her dark eyebrows. 'That makes sense. I would not have expected him to kill himself. And he certainly had plenty of enemies.' She seemed as objective as if she had been a colleague, one of the small but increasing number of female detective inspectors, giving the proposition her objective assessment and approval.

110

Lambert tried and failed to hide the irritation he felt at this mantle of composure. 'So which of these many enemies do you think blew his head away, Mrs Berridge?'

She looked at him, acknowledging the brutality of the phrase, knowing how she had provoked it. There was no smile upon her lips, but there was perhaps a look of satisfaction in her eyes, which were of so dark a blue that they looked black, except when she turned to the light of the window. He was reminded of an opponent who made a telling chess move and waited to see the effect upon the player across the table. She took a sip of her coffee, apparently found it satisfactory, and said, 'I have no idea who might have killed him. I suspect that you know far more of his business dealings than I do. I took care to know less and less as the years went on.'

'That was no doubt very wise of you, from a personal point of view.' But you didn't spurn his ill-gotten gains, he thought; without leaving her face, his eyes took in a peripheral view of the wide acreage of fitted carpet and the huge picture windows which lined the wall of the penthouse. 'Your ignorance is, of course, rather distressing from the point of view of officers investigating his murder. I ask you again: have you any idea who might have killed your husband?'

He expected a denial to spring too quickly from those wide lips; that would have denoted a refusal even to think about the question. Instead, she switched her gaze from his face and cast it for a moment upon the long low table, where a tiny wraith of steam rose from the mouth of the coffee pot. Eventually she said calmly, 'I should like to help you, because I do not approve of murder, even when . . . well, even when the victim has perhaps invited it by his own conduct. But I'm afraid I cannot. My guess is that it might be a rival from the murky waters in which he moved.'

The prospect of having to trawl through the filthy pool of urban gangland had already occurred to Lambert. A contract killer who knew his business was the most difficult of all murderers to trap. And there were an increasing number of them operating in Britain, as the stakes in the rival drug and club empires grew ever higher. But they did not often act on a man's home ground, especially in a semi-rural area like this, where the chances of anonymity were reduced. In the face of the widow's coolness, he retreated behind statistics. 'The overwhelming probability in a killing like this is that the victim was killed by someone who knew him well.'

'I see.' She looked interrogatively at Bert Hook, then leaned across to refill his Royal Worcester cup. The movement might have been designed to show off the suppleness of her body; her back arched gracefully and the cashmere sweater was pulled tight across firm, full breasts. She swung her torso effortlessly and effectively, refilling Lambert's empty cup without troubling to consult him. This time her hand seemed steady, as if she had gathered strength from what had gone on thus far. 'I'm afraid I still cannot offer any useful suggestions.'

She seemed to him now to be taunting his skill as an interrogator with body language as well as her facial expressions. He said, 'You were missing yesterday when we tried to contact you, Mrs Berridge. Where were you?'

There was a spark of open aggression in her glance as she looked full into his face again. 'I didn't kill him, you know.'

'No one has accused you of that. But you will surely understand that we need to know where you were at the time of the death.'

She nodded, as if she was accepting a new line of argument rather than something which must always have been obvious to her. There was still no sign of emotion as she asked, 'When was he killed?'

He had no intention of telling her that, until she had released more of her own thoughts to him. 'I saw him myself at about six o'clock on Tuesday evening. And we found him dead at eleven-fifty-two on Wednesday morning. He died at some time in those eighteen hours.'

She looked at him, sizing him up, weighing him as an adversary. 'But you know more accurately than that, by now. You just don't intend to tell me what you know. Is that the usual police procedure?'

112

He ignored her question and the taunt in its phrasing. 'Where were you in those hours, Mrs Berridge?'

The muscles around her mouth and nose tightened. Now that the moment for which she had prepared herself could be put off no longer, she seemed after all a little nervous. 'I went out early on Tuesday evening. I was – visiting a friend.'

Bert Hook had at last something to enter in his notebook. He looked at her over the top of it and said, 'At what time would this be, Mrs Berridge?'

'I left here at six o'clock.' The answer had come a little too quickly, not just on the heels of his question but almost before he had completed it. 'We met in Stratford, you see. We went to the evening performance at the Royal Shakespeare Theatre.'

Lambert said, 'And what was the play on Tuesday night?'

She gave him a tiny smile, acknowledging the swiftness of his reaction, ready with her response. 'It was *The Winter's Tale*, Superintendent. We thoroughly enjoyed it.'

'And you returned here afterwards?'

'No.' Again the answer came too quickly, swift and abrupt as a rifle shot behind his question. She made a visible effort to relax. 'I stayed overnight in Stratford.'

'That seems a little unusual. It can scarcely be more than fifty miles from here.'

'I often spend the night away from here.' Her pause invited them to diversify, but neither policeman took up the bait. 'I – I wanted to see a little more of my friend. We'd scarcely had time to talk, you see. We had to get into the theatre as soon as we met.'

Bert Hook said quietly, 'We shall need the name of this friend, of course.' They were a good pair, these two men, each understanding the moves the other required of him from long practice. He poised his ball-pen expectantly over the page.

She looked from one to the other, finding only that the watchful faces were united against her. 'Can I rely on your discretion?'

Lambert tried to prevent his irritation with the woman coming out as truculence. 'Only if this proves to have no bearing on the case. You must surely see that we need con-firmation of your movements during this period, if we are to clear you of suspicion.'

'Part of the routine again, I suppose.' She tried to tease him with the repetition of his earlier phrase, but it fell flat against the seriousness of her position. 'All right. I was with a man.'.

'Name?' Hook was impassive as an Oriental over his notebook.

'Mr Faraday.' The name sounded oddly in her ears; she thought it was the first time she had ever given him the title.

'Mr Ian Faraday?' Lambert tried not to reveal the clankings of his brain as various things about the attitude of Faraday before the killing fell into place for him.

Gabrielle nodded. She found that it was after all a relief that it was out at last. They had known it must be so, when they had prepared together for this interview and the one he would have in turn. 'Ian and I will be getting married, when all this is over.'

Unless one of you is serving a life sentence, thought Lambert. He said only, 'We shall need full details of your meeting with Mr Faraday, of course. When you met, how long you were together, whether either of you left the other for any substantial period. And the name of anyone who can witness that you were together for the time you claim.'

'We met in Stratford at seven o'clock. Went to the theatre as I said. We'd booked into the River Crescent Hotel, but we went for a drink after the theatre. I suppose it must have been about half past eleven when we got into the hotel.'

'The receptionist will be able to confirm that time?'

'Yes. Well, Mr Allan, actually, the proprietor. It's only a small place. We've stayed there before, so he knows us.' The answers were coming quickly, with no hesitation between the phrases. This was information that had been ready for delivery. But that might have been no more than the prudence of the innocent.

Lambert said, 'You say you were at the theatre during the evening. Can you provide any evidence of that?'

This time she paused, furrowed her brow, gave every

evidence of cudgelling her brain. Perhaps, he thought sourly, she had noticed her earlier haste in delivery. Her face brightened. 'I think I have the programme for *The Winter's Tale.*' She rose and went over to the corner of the room, where the top of a glossy cover protruded from a leather bag. 'Yes. Here it is.' She handed it across the table, trying not to produce the effect of a conjuror delivering back the card originally chosen.

Lambert glanced at the cover, then put the programme down on the coffee table; with its elaborate cover design, detailing the rural delights of the play's middle section, it sat there rather appropriately, as if it had become part of the design of this huge and elegant room. 'And would anyone in the theatre be able to remember seeing you? The programme-seller? A barman at the interval?' It sounded churlish, but at this moment courtesy was the least of his concerns.

For an instant, she looked frightened. But her voice was even enough as she said, 'I doubt it. The theatre was full, as usual. There was a queue for programmes, and you know what a crush there is in the bar at the interval.'

He did indeed; he had given up all hope of a drink in the same theatre only a month ago. 'So you spent the night at this hotel. And what did you do yesterday? We were trying to contact you from lunch-time onwards.'

Was it imagination, or did she relax? Certainly she smiled, as if she felt that the important period was now accounted for, though he had refused to reveal to her when that was. 'We spent the morning in Stratford, then drove out to Broadway for lunch. We called at the National Trust garden at Hidcote in the afternoon. I expect I may have the tickets in here.' She fumbled in the bag and produced the tickets. He looked at the edge and saw the previous day's date clearly printed there.

'And no doubt during all this time you knew nothing of your husband's death?'

'No. I drove back here in my own car at about six. I didn't know there was anything wrong until I saw your plastic tapes cutting off access to my husband's garage and the constable on duty there. George Lewis told me about Jim's death.'

115

It held together, as far as it went, better than many alibis offered by innocent people. He wondered a little about the theatre visit, but she had provided all they could reasonably expect. If it was true, the dead man's widow and Faraday alibied each other. Two prime subjects eliminated immediately: he should have been pleased about that. Instead, he was reluctant to concede yet that it was so. He said, 'How long have you and Mr Faraday had this association?'

'Over a year now. My marriage to James was over long before this began. He has – had lots of women. I gave up worrying about them years ago. I thought at first that I was just having a fling with Ian – perhaps even just getting back at James. It developed into something deeper.' She was earnest about this, wanting to convince him of her seriousness, like a young lover. He knew suddenly that there had been very few affairs, perhaps none, for her before this one.

'Mr Faraday was an employee of Berridge Limited. Were you not afraid of your husband's reaction if he found out about this liaison?'

She nodded. Apparently she was as ready to talk about this as she had been reluctant to give them the information they needed earlier. 'We were very frightened. James was both vindictive and vicious, as you no doubt know. He would have got rid of Ian and done his best to prevent him getting another job, for a start – and perhaps much worse. I don't know how he'd have punished me, but he'd have found a way. But it wasn't too difficult to deceive him. He was away a lot of the time, and he'd long since stopped caring much about what I did.' She paused, then smiled a curious, elated smile. 'I was about to set about getting a divorce from James. That won't be necessary, now.'

'You know how your husband was killed?'

For a moment, she looked alarmed, as if he was accusing her of witnessing that violent moment. Then she understood him and nodded. 'Yes. He was shot at close quarters. They explained that to me at the mortuary, before they let me see the body.'

'Do you know if your husband possessed a firearm?'

'Yes, he did. He kept a gun in his desk.'

116

Like most non-users, she was unaware of the correct distinctions. 'A pistol?'

'Yes. He had it in the top drawer of his desk.'

'Was it a Smith and Wesson .357?'

'I think that was the name, yes. The number means nothing to me.'

'A pistol was found by the body. Very probably the one we have just described. We may need to ask you to identify it, in due course.' There was no record of Berridge having a licence for the pistol, but that was rather what he would have expected. 'Where did he keep this pistol?'

'I told you, in his desk. In the top right-hand drawer, I think. I haven't seen it since we moved in here.'

'Yet you knew of its existence.'

'Yes. James showed it to me when he first got it. He was the kind of man who liked the trappings of violence. He wanted me to know that he had it. It only replaced another, less powerful gun.'

'When?'

She thought for a moment, completely at ease in discussing the instrument which had in all probability dispatched her husband from the world. 'About two years ago, I think. I couldn't be sure, but it was at about the time when we moved in here.'

'And as far as you know it was in the desk until the time of your husband's death?'

'Yes. I certainly wouldn't have touched it – I can't stand the things. And he kept the drawer locked.'

They left then, with instructions that she should not disappear again without letting them know of her whereabouts. 'More of the routine, I expect,' she said, teasing them a little now that it was over. The sergeant smiled at her, thanked her politely for the coffee.

She watched the old Vauxhall turn out of the car park and convey them slowly down the drive. Once they were safely on their way, she would ring Ian and report. The very tall one, the superintendent, had been sticky at first. But on the whole, it had gone as well as could be expected, she thought. That would be a relief to Ian. She pictured his anxious, vulnerable face and wished she could be with him. But she knew they must be patient and careful for a while longer.

She gathered up the coffee cups and took them into the kitchen. As she washed them, she reflected on how the one, very necessary, lie had led on to others.

# 15

The men who had killed Charlie Pegg were left in separate cells for three hours in the Oldford nick.

They were hard men, who had endured this treatment and worse before, but it had its effect. Even men without much imagination find that uncertainty creeps in when they are left to sweat it out alone. They never admit it, of course, but the effects are there to see for their guardians, studying them at intervals like goldfish in a bowl. After three hours, Sturley and Jones were feeling more like rats in a trap.

They were on a murder rap. That was what was new. They had killed before, more than once, but the pigs had never got close to pinning them down. This time it was all to be different, and over three hours that realization gradually sank in. Like most men who dish out physical violence from positions of strength, they were cowards at heart. That meant that they had scant resources to deal with this new situation.

It was Sturley, the more intelligent of the two, who was brought up first. They let him stew for another ten minutes in the airless interview room with its single high light behind the wire cage. Then Rushton came to him with Hook, the two of them grimly confident, the memory of Sturley's victim lying dead in the gutter as their stimulus.

Rushton brought an excitement, a grim anticipation of pleasure, with him into the tiny room. Policemen are human, and the prospect of bullying a bully appealed to him. He looked at the big, raw-boned face opposite him and said, 'So it's come to this at last. A murder rap.'

'I don't know what you're talking about. You're trying to fit me up. I want my brief.' There was a pause between each of the sentences, as Sturley waited for a reaction. He got none; the result was that his attempted truculence rang increasingly hollow. They heard him out with apparent interest, even looked surprised when he failed to offer more.

Then Rushton said, 'The one you asked for seems to be no longer available. We're still trying, of course, but Jim Berridge's empire seems to have collapsed with him.' They would know about Berridge's death by now, but all the media reports had implied it was a suicide by a man about to be arrested: the police press relations officer had done a good job.

Sturley muttered, 'I want Flynn. No one else.' It was the formula they had been told to mouth, if they were ever arrested. He was not sure whether it still applied, now that Berridge had gone, but he did not know what other tactic to adopt.

'And you shall have him. If he's still in the country. If he still wishes to act for scum like you. If he thinks you will be able to pay him, now that the Berridge umbrella is removed.' Rushton took an unopened packet of cigarettes out of his jacket pocket, watched Sturley's eyes switch to it like a starving child's, then returned it casually whence it had come. 'You're going to need a good brief this time, aren't you, Sturley? But you'll find he'll have to confine himself to mitigating circumstances, and he'll find precious few of those.' He contemplated the bear of a man across the table, noting with satisfaction the damp beneath the arms of his T-shirt, savouring the scent of the sweat upon him as if it were an exotic perfume.

Sturley, who had been determined three hours ago to say nothing, now said grudgingly, 'If you're still on about Charlie Pegg, you can go stuff yourself. You've got nothing on us for that one.'

Even the mention of Pegg was a sign of weakness, and all three men in the room recognized it. It was Hook who now leaned forward and said, 'Funny. That isn't what your mate says.' His smile was positively Machiavellian; it would have shocked those young colleagues of his who thought of him

120

as an old-fashioned village bobby who had somehow strayed into CID work.

Sturley glanced sharply at this new and unexpected source of torment. He said, 'Jonesey wouldn't talk.' But where he had meant there to be confidence, there was anxiety in his tone. They caught that doubt, and smiled at him. He longed to leap forward, to smash his great fists into those smug faces, to feel the breaking skin and raw flesh beneath his knuckles, to shout his hatred and move in with the boot once they were down. But he knew he could not, and with the removal of that physical outlet he felt the weakness creeping through his limbs.

Hook said, 'Quite a little talker, your pal Jonesey, when he gets going. He surprised me: I didn't think he had that many words in him. But he was scared, you see. You know how that makes men shout for mercy.'

Sturley did. He had heard the pleas of desperate men often enough, as they had fallen under his blows. But he had never heeded them, and that realization filled him now with something like despair. These pigs had wanted to have him like this for a long time now, and they too would not show mercy. He was profoundly worried about what his companion might have said. Jones had always taken his lead from Sturley, had been contented to be a brutal and effective second string throughout the years of intimidation and violence which had been so lucrative for them as Berridge's empire grew. Left on his own, he would be uncertain.

Sturley searched wretchedly for some of his original defiance. 'You can't pin Charlie Pegg on to us. No weapon. No connection with us.' He looked from one to the other of the officers, willing one of them, either of them, to give him some sort of response.

Instead, they watched him in silence for a few moments, fancying that they could smell the fear now amidst the man's sweat, knowing that they had the thing which would confound him. It was Rushton who said eventually, like one patiently offering instruction, 'No. We do not have a weapon. You may choose to tell us at some later time just where it was that you dumped it. But there is at any murder scene what we like to call an "exchange" between the victim and his killers. With the benefits of modern science, we find that murderers leave something of themselves behind, however careful they think they have been. I'm delighted to tell you that you and Jonesey did that, Sturley.'

'I don't believe you. It's all balls!' But there was doubt now in his voice, where he had intended contempt.

'It isn't balls, Sturley. Your mate Jones was a little careless, you see. He let Pegg claw at him as he went down, I expect. There was a little blood on Charlie's body that wasn't his own, you see. Not much, compared with what Charlie shed. Just a smear. But enough. The DNA boys were delighted with their tests. Not too bright, your mate Jonesey, after all.'

'It's bollocks! It's all part of your – '

'And fibres, Sturley. Your mate left fibres. Not many, but enough. On poor old Charlie's left shoulder and neck.' Rushton produced a sheet from the inside pocket of his lightweight grey jacket, opened it with deliberation, consulted it, registered satisfaction as he found the detail he wanted. 'Matched with the fibres of socks found in the flat of Walter Jones.'

Rushton put the sheet away and looked back at Sturley. Then he changed his delivery, so that the words spat like bullets across the table. 'Couldn't resist the odd kick when your man was down, could he, your mate? Pity he didn't get rid of the socks where you threw the knife you stabbed with, wasn't it? But then you buggers are never as bright as you like to think you are.'

He let his disgust pour across the table, up and over the huge, waxy face with its eyes filling with fear. He had won. He was savouring the moment, anticipating the final collapse.

Sturley wondered wildly whether to deny that he had been there, to put it all on Jones. But he knew he could never make that stick. Jones would tell them, insist upon it, even if he hadn't done so already. As if to toll the knell of his hopes, Hook said, 'John Murray, the manager at the Curvy Cats, has already blown your alibi. He's admitted you were away from the club at the time of Pegg's death. Once Berridge is removed, everyone is suddenly prepared to talk, you see.

It's a rotten old world.' Hook's expression said that at this moment he found this world entirely satisfying.

Sturley looked from one to the other. He said, 'Jonesey's a stupid bastard. He should never have opened his mouth to pigs.' It produced no reaction from the men opposite him; they all knew that it was irrelevant now. 'All right. We were acting on Berridge's orders. We had no option. We only did what he asked us to do. We didn't even know what Pegg had done.'

It was the old, useless defence of obeying orders. It wouldn't do him any good, but there was no point in telling him that. They had what they wanted. They told him about the statement he would sign. He nodded, defeated, eyes cast down, massive shoulders bowed. They released him then, had him escorted back to his cell.

The success was a bond between two officers who were temperamentally opposed. For a moment they were close. And in the future years, the gap between them would be reduced a tiny but tangible fraction by their memory of this success.

They looked at each other for a moment, smiled a tight little agreement. Rushton said to the desk sergeant, 'You can have Jones brought up now. We'll see what he has to say for himself.'

Ian Faraday's house had the depressing untidiness of a man who lives alone. It was neither dirty nor chaotic. There were no dishes in the sink, though the stacking drainer beside it was two-thirds full of the crockery which had been there for two days. There were two packets of cereals on the breakfast bar in the kitchen, which were probably never put away into one of the oak-fronted units.

The lounge into which the sales director led Lambert and Hook was clinically clean compared with some of the squalid rooms they had to enter in the course of their work. But there was a thin film of dust visible upon the china ornaments on the windowsill, and one of the drawers in the sideboard against the wall was slightly open. Yesterday's newspaper still lay where it had fallen, beside what was obviously the only armchair in regular use. The chair was out of alignment with the rest of the three-piece suite; it had been turned to face the television in the corner of the room. The companion of the man who lives alone, thought Lambert. He wondered suddenly if Chris Rushton's house was like this now, if, indeed, he was coping as well as this. Lambert had only been there once, and in those days the place had had the imprint of a competent young woman and the happy chaos of a toddler.

Faraday said nervously, 'I hope you didn't mind coming here. Policemen appearing at the office cause a lot of gossip, and we can do without that at the moment. There was enough talk when you came to see me on your own the other day.'

Lambert nodded. 'And that was before your employer was murdered. A visit in connection with a murder investigation would only excite the natives even more. We are aware of the disturbances we cause, but they will be inevitable, I'm afraid, as long as there are serious crimes. Did our officer come in to get your fingerprints?'

Faraday nodded. He did not seem to think it strange that he should be included among the group who might have been around the scene of the murder. 'He explained that it was just for elimination purposes.'

They had not yet been asked to sit down. Hook was looking through the patio doors at the back garden, which showed the same signs of partial neglect as the house set upon it as spring advanced. The lawn had been mown, but the edges were not cut. The roses were springing into growth, but they had not been pruned, and the tallest of them had been bent low by a gale, towards the ground where the weeds were beginning to burgeon. Faraday must have caught his glance, for he said, 'I used to be quite keen on the garden. But I don't seem to get the time now, and I must admit that for a lot of the time it scarcely seems worth the effort.'

With no one to show it off to, it wouldn't, thought Lambert. He was suddenly grateful for the cosy domesticity which sometimes seemed so dull. He would make an effort to enjoy his extended family to the full this weekend, when Caroline and the grandchildren arrived. He sat down on the sofa which had seen so little recent use; Hook joined him and Faraday turned the armchair from the television to face them.

Lambert said, 'We are checking the movements of people who were close to Jim Berridge in relation to the time of his death. We already know something of your actions at that time, Mr Faraday, but we need confirmation from you. And a little more information.'

He had not meant it to sound threatening, but it emerged so. Faraday took a deep breath and uttered the words he had determined on whilst he waited for them to arrive. 'I should make one thing clear. I was not close to Jim Berridge, except when he came into our offices, which wasn't very often. The more I saw of him, the less I liked him.'

'In view of what we know about him, that can only be to your credit. We shall be checking how far, if at all, you were involved in his criminal activities in due course.' All their information so far indicated that Faraday's only involvement was with the legitimate woollens and men's shop businesses which Berridge had used as a front for his seamier dealings. But there was no need to concede that at this point; it was better to keep their man hopping about on his back foot, as former fast bowler Bert Hook usually put it.

It was Hook, who had so far confined himself to making great play with his notebook preparations, who now said, 'And Berridge had no reason to like you, had he, Mr Faraday? You were conducting an affair with his wife.'

Faraday had always thought privately of the liaison as reflecting credit upon him: it took a brave man to risk an affair with the boss's wife, particularly when that boss was Jim Berridge. He had been surprised over the months by his own audacity. Now his actions had landed him in the position of a murder suspect. For the first time, he realized how serious a suspect he must be, from the point of view of these men. He said, 'Fortunately, Jim didn't know about Gabrielle and me. I shudder to think what he might have done to us if he had discovered it.' Almost comically on cue, he was shaken by a small, involuntary shiver at the thought.

125

Lambert said, 'But now he never will know, so you need no longer contend with that possibility.'

Ian had been congratulating himself on that for a day and more. Now, emerging from the mouth of someone else, what had been a relief seemed like a threat to his security. He said, 'You're saying that gives me a motive for his murder?'

'Oh, we're more concerned with facts than motivation, at this stage. No use pinning down a perfect motive and then discovering the chap couldn't possibly have done it because he was somewhere else at the time.' He smiled a little, studying Faraday's broad-set eyes beneath the abundant crop of brown hair, speculating about the workings of the brain behind them.

'Quite. And I was somewhere else on the night when Berridge died. Fifty miles away.' Ian smiled, even managed to look confident: he was, after all, a successful salesman.

This time, Lambert did not return the smile. Instead, he said quickly, 'Who told you when Berridge died, Mr Faraday? The death has been placed between six on Tuesday evening and eleven-fifty-two on Wednesday morning. We have not yet released any more definite time than that.'

Faraday's mouth opened; his smile dived away into the cavity as swiftly as a startled lizard. 'I – I thought . . . I suppose I just assumed he had been killed at night. Dead of night, and that sort of image, I suppose.' The throwaway laugh he attempted did not sound convincing, even to himself.

'Hmm. Mrs Berridge seemed to be making the same assumption. Interesting, that.'

Ian waited for them to enlarge on this, even to press him on the mistake he had made. Anything suddenly seemed an improvement on this stretching silence, in which his temple thumped and his brain obstinately refused to work. Eventually, he said rather desperately, 'Anyway, I was away overnight, in Stratford. With Gabrielle. We went to the Royal Shakespeare Theatre. I expect she told you that.'

'She did indeed. *The Winter's Tale*, I believe. Mrs Berridge showed us the programme.'

Ian wished they would not keep calling her that. It was

126

an unwelcome insistence on a connection he wished to oblit-erate as swiftly as possible. He said irrelevantly, 'We shall be getting married, in due course.' Then he wished immediately that he had kept quiet. It seemed to bind him even more closely to the murder of the man who had stood in the way of this alliance.

As if in response to that thought, Lambert said, 'Sergeant Hook will take the details of your movements last night.'

'I think Gabrielle has told you the essentials already.'

Hook said, 'We need them from you, Mr Faraday.'

'To see if our accounts agree?'

'Any discrepancies between them would certainly be of great interest to us.' When Bert Hook was scrupulously polite, it was always a danger signal, thought Lambert.

Faraday licked his lips. 'Well, I was here for a couple of hours after I saw you on Tuesday afternoon, Mr Lambert. I suppose I left here at about six. I met Gabrielle in Stratford just before the performance. I couldn't be sure of the time, but it must have been about twenty past seven. We just had time to buy a programme and get to our seats.'

'And where did you meet?'

For a moment, he looked lost; perhaps it was just a genuine difficulty in recalling the exact point of their rendezvous. 'Outside the theatre. We knew we wouldn't have a lot of time to spare before the play, you see.'

The explanation was an unnecessary gloss, an attempt to justify where none was needed. Gabrielle Berridge had told them that they had met at seven, and by the Shakespeare memorial. There were discrepancies of twenty minutes and two hundred yards in Faraday's account of their rendezvous; interesting, but perhaps not wide enough to be significant.

'Do you think anyone on the theatre staff will remember you?'

Faraday shook his head. 'I've thought about that. I should think it's unlikely. The place was full, and the bars were crowded at the interval.'

'And afterwards?'

'We had a drink at the Swan. It was crowded, as you would expect at that time. I got the drinks at the bar, but I doubt if the girl who served me would remember it – she was run off her feet at the time.'

He gave every appearance of a man genuinely trying to be helpful. Lambert studied him for a moment, wondering whether the man would realize the crucial nature of his next question.

Faraday sat with legs crossed in his armchair. His lightly patterned shirt and tie were both expensive and fashionable, no doubt products of the business he represented. His suit was a well-cut dark-brown worsted, his shoes in supple burgundy leather. There was certainly anxiety in the brown eyes beneath the plentiful crop of well-groomed hair, but that was natural enough: they had made it abundantly clear that he was at the centre of a murder investigation.

Lambert said, 'Have you anything which would prove conclusively that you attended the theatre on Tuesday evening?'

'I thought you said that Gabrielle had found the programme for you?'

'She did indeed. Without much difficulty. But perhaps you are not aware that programmes do not relate to a particular performance. At the Royal Shakespeare Theatre, you can even buy them in the theatre during the day, when no performance is taking place.'

'I see. I hadn't considered that.' Faraday pondered the matter, then reached into his pocket. When he failed to locate what he wanted there, he said, 'Other jacket, I think. Bear with me for a moment.' He rose and strode swiftly from the room, as if action was a relief to him. They heard his feet hurrying up the stairs, then boards creaked briefly over their heads. In less than a minute, he was back with them, trying not to look too pleased with his find. 'Will these be of any use? They're the ticket stubs from Tuesday night. I see they've got the date and time of the performance on them.'

'That should certainly be most useful.' Bert Hook spoke stiffly, feeling that this was a play in which he deserved better lines. He took the rather grubby stubs, checked the information, made a note of their details on his pad, then returned them to their owner.

They took the name of the small hotel where Faraday had

spent the night with Gabrielle Berridge, then listened to his account of their movements on the next day. It conformed exactly with what she had told them. As she had done, he seemed to relax as he retailed the places and the times, as though he knew as clearly as they did that the crisis period was on the previous night and now accounted for.

In fifteen minutes, they were back in the murder room at Oldford CID. Rushton had news for them. 'Report's come in from Forensic on the murder weapon. Prints from Berridge's right hand on it.'

'None from the left hand?' Lambert was thinking of how he would put this in his report for the Coroner.

'No.' Rushton looked at the Ceefax. 'Rather indicates that the victim's hand was put on the handle after he was shot, they say. Looks as if the pistol had been wiped clear of all other prints and the killer wore gloves. That's no more than we expected. But there is one interesting thing. There is a single print from someone else on the butt of the pistol.'

'Who?' Trust Rushton to hold back the interesting item, thought Lambert.

'We don't know yet. I've got two DCs going through records, but we haven't turned up anyone yet. They've only been on it for about twenty minutes, but it shouldn't take long to do a scan, with modern technology.' He put the little plug for progress in automatically.

'But the print could be from one of the people we're interviewing.'

'It could indeed. They've all allowed their dabs to be taken, but we haven't had them processed and compared yet. But we should know in a few hours if it was one of them. Of course, it could be a contract killer. There are several of them that we do not have prints for, because they have never been identified.'

But a professional would never be so naïve as to leave a print behind, thought Lambert. With any luck at all, this was going to be one of their suspects.

# 16

Lambert, driving alone into Old Mead Park, decided that all new blocks of flats should have resident porters.

They were a great addition to security in themselves. And when a crime did take place, they were as useful as two extra members of a CID team. At least, they were if George Lewis was typical. His knowledge of the habits of the residents made it possible to eliminate most of them from suspicion, for he was able to confirm much of what they said individually to the door-to-door team. And his intimate knowledge of the building and of the interiors of many of the apartments was at the disposal of the police.

Lewis had assumed an interest in CID work from the moment when he heard of the violent death of his old friend Charlie Pegg. There was no humbug about Lewis. Once he knew of Berridge's involvement in that death, he made no secret of his satisfaction at the violent death of this most affluent of his residents. Whatever the motivation behind this killing, George Lewis took it as just retribution for the dispatch of his friend.

Lambert now took steps to secure his continuing co-operation by giving him welcome news. 'Sturley and Jones have been charged with the murder of Charlie this morning, George. And it will stick. They've virtually confessed now. Pleading that they were under orders from Berridge.'

'They were, weren't they?' Lewis was anxious to have all the details of what had happened to Pegg clear in his mind.

'Yes, Berridge was certainly the ultimate murderer. But those gorillas were his instruments. They'll go down for a long time, don't you worry about that.'

Lewis nodded, a small, rotund figure who yet acquired a surprising dignity in his concern for his dead friend. 'If Berridge killed him, then I'm glad he died the way he did. He didn't deserve anything better.'

'I understand that you should feel that, George. I've been after Berridge for too long to shed any tears over him now. But I think you will understand that we can't have people taking the law into their own hands. I still have to find out who killed him.'

The porter considered the proposition, saw the logic of the argument, shrugged his reluctance to accept it. 'I suppose so. But I'm not a policeman. So personally, I hope whoever killed him gets away with it. I went to see Amy Pegg last night. She's still devastated by what happened to Charlie. The two of them should have been able to look forward to a decent retirement.' He spoke with the vehemence of deep feeling. Then, as if he thought such passion indecorous within a porter's uniform, he said with a sudden bathos, 'He was a good workman, Charlie. Better than people expected.'

Lambert realized that it was true: he had been surprised by the quality of the craftsmanship in the units Pegg had installed in the penthouse above them. He said gently, 'Charlie wasn't an angel. He spied a bit on people, you know, George. It may even have been that that led to his death, for all we know.'

He thought Lewis might have defended his friend or professed ignorance. Instead, the porter said, 'I guessed that. From what you asked me about his notebook, when you came here after his death. He was always a nosey little bugger!' It was said with affection. Lewis looked out of the window of his office, seeing not the vista outside, but the world he had inhabited with Charlie Pegg thirty years and more ago. 'He could tell you scandal about anyone in our company in Cyprus, when he trusted you. But he kept it mostly to himself. And he was useful to you, Mr Lambert.'

The last sentence, as Lewis pulled himself back to the present, was almost an accusation. And with some justification: Pegg would still have been alive if he hadn't chosen to act as a police snout. But CID men had to take help wherever they could find it, and Pegg had known the dangers. Lambert said gently, 'He was paid for the help he gave, George. But I'm sorry he died, and I'm glad we got the men who did it. That won't stop me from following up the murder of James Berridge. Now, it appears that Berridge was killed with his own weapon. Did you ever see him with a pistol?'

'No. He was much too smooth for that. He always presented the image of the successful business tycoon round here.' That was a common enough pattern. It was often the biggest villains who took care to be eminently, even excessively, respectable when away from the scenes of their crimes.

'You know the layout of the penthouse upstairs?'

'Yes. Better than almost any of the other flats. I've been here from the start, you see, and the Berridges had quite a lot of extra fittings put in. I was in and out with the workmen. Mrs Berridge was happy to leave it to me – she wasn't around that much, even in the old days.'

Lambert noted that last phrase. He said quietly, 'In the days before Mr Faraday came on the scene, you mean?' He saw the hesitation in the smooth face above the uniform. 'This is a murder enquiry, George. You'd much better be completely honest.'

Lewis smiled ruefully, as though he was grateful for the reminder of his duty. 'Yes, I realized there was something going on. He came here to pick up Mrs Berridge occasionally, no doubt when he was sure that there was no chance of his boss being around. It was Charlie who confirmed it for me, though.'

'And how did he know about it?'

'I'm not sure. He only mentioned it because he thought I knew about it. And I suppose I did, really. He just confirmed it.'

'The Berridges have an answerphone. Did Charlie listen to the messages recorded on it?'

Lewis looked uneasy, as if the dead man's inquisitive behaviour somehow reflected on him. 'I think he probably did, now. Both in the penthouse and in one or two of the other flats that had those things. But it's only since you spoke to me about all those initials in his notebook that I realized

132

that. I would have slung him out if I'd known at the time, friend or not.'

'I'm sure you would, George. Now. Where did Berridge keep this pistol of his?'

'I — I don't know. I told you, I never saw it.' He looked anxious, as though he feared they might not believe him. 'I think he might have kept it in the top drawer of his desk, in his study, but I don't know for sure.'

It was the second time Lambert had been told the weapon was kept in that drawer. Who had removed it? He said, 'What makes you think he kept it there, George?'

Lewis looked uncomfortable. 'I checked that room, when I let Charlie Pegg into the penthouse to work. Mrs Berridge told me expressly that he wasn't to go into her husband's study, you see. And — well, knowing Charlie's weakness, I went in to check just how secure it was against nosey parkers.' He looked thoroughly embarrassed by his betrayal of his dead friend. 'I tried the drawers, to see if they were locked, you see. That top one was. I suppose when you mentioned a gun I thought immediately that there was where it might have been. But I didn't know that.'

'It's a reasonable enough assumption, if the drawer was locked. Unless he carried it around with him, of course. As a matter of fact, you're probably right. Mrs Berridge also thought that her husband kept a pistol in that top drawer.'

The porter's face lightened, as if that took away from him the responsibility of giving information about the residents, even the worst of residents. Lambert said gently, 'What time did Mrs Berridge leave here on the night of the murder, George?'

Lewis said, 'I told you when you asked me before. I don't know. For all I know, she was gone long before her husband was killed.' It was curiously indefinite phrasing from this straightforward man. He looked away from the superintendent as soon as he had spoken, to the noticeboard he did not need, which listed the names of the residents.

George Lewis understood what the superintendent said about it being his job to uphold the law. But for himself, he still hoped that the killer of James Berridge would not be apprehended.

Gabrielle Berridge drove quickly, but she was in perfect control of her vehicle. The red Mazda sports coupé was immediately responsive, precise in its steering as she placed it into bends, holding the road without any tendency to oversteer. She enjoyed that feeling of unity with the car, of the bonding of driver and machine into an effective unit.

Normally, that is. Today, though she drove swiftly and safely, she did not feel the delight which normally lifted her spirit on the open road. As she approached her destination, she even found herself slowing down, stealing a little more time to organize in her mind what she had thought was already properly planned. Above the first opening buds of the chestnut trees which grew tall in the heart of England, she was conscious of sharp blue sky and flying white clouds. But the spring day seemed to be mocking her mission, as if nature's brightness was emphasizing the pettiness of human duplicity.

She felt now that she could not succeed in this, that the attempt could only lead to humiliation for her. But she had said she would try, so there was no alternative. The tourist traffic was not as heavy as it would be in the summer months, though she saw half a dozen coaches in the car park as she drove over the Avon and into the town. The bunting was out across the Stratford streets for the Shakespeare birthday celebrations, and the town presented a bustling, cheerful front to its visitors. She turned away from the great brick warehouse of a theatre, through the narrow streets round the church where the bard was buried with his mysterious inscription and his bland plaster effigy, like the face of a Victorian industrialist.

Moving ever more slowly, as if she had communicated her reluctance to it, the sleek sports car turned towards where the slow-flowing Avon wound in a huge bend below the town. The streets were quiet here. The houses had the quiet air of discretion which dated from an age before the motor car. Gabrielle composed herself for a moment in the parked car. Then she got out, straightened her blue tartan waist-coat automatically, and went determinedly into the River Crescent Hotel.

To her relief, the man she wanted was behind the desk. He might have been anywhere in the building, for this was only a small private hotel and the proprietor had to be a ubiquitous worker. In the early days of her relationship with Ian Faraday, it had seemed the ideal place to avoid attention. She thought that even in the future, they would favour it against more pretentious establishments, for it had served them well and they would love it because of its memories.

'Good morning, Mr Allan!' she said. She was relieved that her voice did not sound nervous in her own ears.

The smile on the man's face as he looked up was genuine, not professionally assumed. As owner and manager, he enjoyed his work. Neat and affable, unflappable whether on public show to his clients or in the stress of the kitchen at the back of this late-Georgian house, he was in control of the situation. He had worked for twenty years to acquire his own establishment, and he was determined to enjoy everything which went with it.

He meant it when he now exclaimed, 'How nice to see you, Mrs Faraday!' He was certain after yesterday of what he had long suspected, that this was not this striking lady's proper name. But that would make no difference to either the service he offered her or the esteem in which he held her. He looked down at the bookings list in front of him, though he knew by heart which rooms were free. 'We can give you your usual double room for the next two nights, if you want it.'

She smiled awkwardly. This would be the first time she had asked anything of this man outside his trade, and the words would not come naturally to her. 'No, it's not about accommodation this time, Mr Allan. I – I wanted to ask you a bit of a favour.'

'Anything we can do to help, of course.' His smile was as broad as ever, but he was puzzled. This elegant woman had always seemed so sure of herself before, so happy in the time she had spent under his roof. Happiness always brought confidence with it, he thought. Now she was unhappy, and he saw her for the first time anxious, even a little frightened, it seemed. Well, she was a good customer, the kind of considerate guest who made his work a pleasure. He would do what he could for her.

He had been hoping that it would be unconnected with what had happened yesterday. It seemed scarcely possible that this graceful, quietly spoken woman could be involved in anything more serious than a little extra-marital affair. But when Gabrielle said, 'We stayed with you on Tuesday night,' he divined where this was going. Already he was regretting that he was not going to be able to help.

Gabrielle made herself try the line she had thought up on the road from Oldford. 'I don't know if you guessed it, Mr Allan, but Mr Faraday is not in fact my husband.' He shrugged a little, implying that he was a man of the world and these things were to be expected. She wished he would speak, but he did not. 'Well, for reasons I won't go into now, it's important to us that we can establish that we were in Stratford quite early on Tuesday evening.'

Though he never looked down at them, he was conscious of her fingers twisting on the handles of the black leather handbag, a tiny gesture which made him at once aware of how important this was for her, and of how sharply sorry he was for her. Merely because he felt her willing him to speak, he said, 'You came here after the theatre. That would establish that you were in the town by seven-thirty. Isn't that early enough?'

She smiled, grateful for the sympathy she felt in his tone. 'It would be, but I get the impression they want some sort of proof.'

Neither of them defined who 'they' were. He said, 'Well, there's your booking for the night recorded in our register.'

'Yes. I – I was wondering . . . Could you say that we popped in here briefly before we went to the theatre? Just to dump our overnight things, you see. As we've done on other occasions. It's suddenly become important for us, you see. We didn't think it would be at the time. It's far too complicated to explain, but I –'

'I would have done what I could, certainly.' It was safe to offer such assurances, now that they could not be tested. 'But I've already told them Mr Faraday booked in by telephone, during Tuesday evening. I said I couldn't remember the exact time. I suppose it must have been after the performance at the theatre.'

'Told whom?' Gabrielle felt suddenly cold.

'The police came here yesterday, Mrs Faraday.' He thought when her face froze that she was going to faint. 'Do sit down, Mrs Faraday. I'll get you some coffee.' He seemed doomed to go on repeating that name which she had acknowledged now was false, as though he was deliberately taunting her.

She let him take her to the chair by the round mahogany table, but she would not let him escape to the kitchen. 'What time did you tell them that we came here?'

'It was a uniformed constable.' He just managed to prevent himself from tacking on that 'Mrs Faraday' again. 'Just a routine check, he said. I told him you didn't get here until half an hour before midnight.'

# 17

One long wall of the travel agency shop was completely lined with the racks of brochures. Members of the public immersed themselves in these, with that concentration characteristic of the English when they are afraid that someone may try to sell them something. Behind the continuous surface of desk which ran down the other side of the room, three women of different ages tapped busily at their computers, recording and digesting the information which became instantly available to them from all over the country.

It was a large room, which had once been two. It was long and narrow, with the only natural light coming from the high-street window where some of the more popular foreign package holidays were displayed as bargains. At the rear of the area, strong neon lighting was necessary to ensure that the golden beaches and the azure seas were allowed to make their full effects.

In the small room behind this emporium of activity, the manager was being questioned about very different things. After the brilliance of the room in which the public moved, this small cell was a surprise. It seemed an odd setting for the chicly dressed figure who sat down before the CID men. Sarah Farrell had plans to turn it into a cosy rest room, but business had been too brisk since she had come here in the autumn for them to give it much attention. It was square and austerely furnished; the curtains were due for replacement and the walls for a coat of paint. The single light bulb above the small table had been given a new shade, but it provided only a dim illumination.

But perhaps Sarah Farrell had chosen the place for the

paucity of its lighting. She had made herself up as carefully as a courtesan to receive them, but it still did not work. As soon as she had seated the two large men on the stand chairs, Lambert said, 'That looks a nasty bang on your eye. Have you let a doctor see it?'

She had thought that even if he noticed it he might ignore it. But he was not an ordinary visitor, and this was not an ordinary conversation. His comment was not only a blow to her self-esteem but an indication of aggression. So there were to be no polite preliminaries in this exchange. She thought of that wine stain on the wall of her cottage, and was glad that she had chosen to meet the police here. These men would not have been deceived by a little rearrangement of the furniture.

She said, 'It's not as bad as it looks. I should have learned by now not to move about in the dark at nights.' She tried the lie oblique, but it seemed no more convincing to her than the lie direct. Perhaps she should have offered no explanation at all.

Lambert smiled a little, not unkindly. 'Did that also bruise your wrist, Miss Farrell?'

She looked down guiltily at the pale skin of her wrist, pulling the cuff of her blouse automatically to cover it, when it was too late. The livid bruising seemed to her to show clearly the imprint of the fingers which had gripped so hard. She thought of the marks they would never see, on her shoulders and back, of the fist in her side which she thought had damaged a rib. Suddenly the deception no longer seemed worthwhile. 'All right. I was knocked about. By a man, of course.'

He looked at the greening of the blackness around her eye, thinking that the timing was about right for a connection with this case, to judge by the development of the injury. Years ago, when he had begun as a beat copper in the East End, sorting out Saturday-night domestic disputes, he had become an expert on 'shiners'. With her blonde hair and white, almost transparent skin, Sarah Farrell was ill equipped to conceal the results of violence. He felt a sudden sympathy for her, when he looked at the efforts she had made with her make-up and saw how ineffective they had been. He said abruptly, 'When was this? And who did it?'

'It was on Tuesday night, after you'd left me at my home. So you can guess who did it.'

'James Berridge, then. You know that he was found dead the next day?'

'Yes.'

'Then you know also why we are here. In a murder enquiry, we have to find out everything we can about the movements of the victim in the last hours before his death.'

She nodded, showing the top of her neatly coiffured blonde head. She had tried at first to pull hair down over her blackened eye, but with the short-cut style that had merely looked ridiculous. Curiously, with the revelation of the truth about her injuries, she felt a welcome composure drop back upon her. In the quiet room, they could just hear the chatter of the computer keyboards from the other side of the wall. She was on her own ground, where people came to her for decisions and she rarely had to hesitate. She was able to give her CID visitors a rueful little smile as she said, 'I've just told you that he knocked me about in the hours before he was murdered. I suppose that's not a good start for me, is it?'

Bert Hook, opening his notebook to record what was to come, tried not to feel too much sympathy for this small, neat figure. The combination of the marks denoting her physical vulnerability and the air of calm competence as she prepared to answer their questions was curiously moving to him. He said, 'You will understand that we need an account of your movements at the time when James Berridge was killed. For elimination purposes, you see.'

'I understand.'

Lambert said, 'That means that we need to know what you did on Tuesday evening between the time I left you and midnight.'

Her blue eyes flashed up and fixed on his, and he saw surprise in them. 'He was killed that night?'

'Sometime before midnight, we think.' There seemed no point now in stretching the possible time of the killing beyond this.

'I'm sorry I tried to protect Jim when you came to my place. He didn't deserve it.'

'No. He was an evil man. I can't regret his removal, but the law says I must investigate his death.' He watched the open, damaged face. James Berridge's mistress didn't seem to be grieving any more than the rest of his acquaintances for him. 'I think you had better tell me what happened after I left your cottage on Tuesday night, Miss Farrell.'

'We had an argument. I tried to question him about the things you'd been asking him about. About the drug dealing. About the murder of that man you said he'd had killed —'

'Charlie Pegg.'

'That's right. Jim told me to shut up and mind my own business. He'd never spoken to me like that before.' She clasped her hands on the lap of her smooth woollen skirt, twisting them as she recollected the dawning horror of that exchange. 'I think I realized at that moment what he really was. It hadn't occurred to me until then how little I knew about him. I'd only known him for a few months, but he'd always treated me kindly; I even thought I mattered a little to him.' She looked for a moment as if she was going to weep; the swollen eyelid fluttered like a technicoloured signal. In the end, she did not dissolve as they thought she would. But it was an effort, and for a moment she could not speak.

Lambert, filling the interval for her, knowing that he must persuade her to continue talking, said quietly, 'It's not unknown, you know. The American gangster bosses often treated women and children close to them kindly, so long as they represented no threat to their criminal activities. Perhaps they found it agreeable to develop another side of their personalities in private. But conscience didn't extend to their business activities.'

He was amazed, as he often was, by the naïvety of females who were otherwise sophisticated and successful women of the world. But then he had known plenty of men do foolish things when sex reared its beguiling head. He wondered if this brisk professional woman had really been as innocent of knowledge about Berridge as she claimed. If Berridge had really knocked her about, that put her one up in Lambert's book. But it also gave her a prime motive for the murder of her assailant. He said, 'Did you ever see Berridge with a pistol?'

Those bright blue eyes were too revealing for the good of their owner. He watched her hesitate about a deception, then decide to tell him the truth. 'Yes. Only once. He had it in the glove box in the car. I was getting a map out when I saw it. But I don't think he minded. It frightened me, but he quite liked to see that. He enjoyed the feeling of power it gave him, I think.'

'Did you ever see him use it?'

'Oh, no. I don't think he had it with him very often. I only saw it on that one occasion. He'd just come back from a meeting in London, I think.'

It was suddenly very important to her that these two large, impassive men believed her. She said, 'The radio bulletin said he was shot in the head. Was it – was it with that gun?'

'We think so, yes.'

He regarded her steadily, watching the idea sink in that she could have gone with him that Tuesday night, could have killed him with that weapon after they had fallen out with each other. Then he said, 'What was it that led up to him hitting you, Miss Farrell?'

The bright blue eyes looked hard at him for a moment. At that moment, Sarah Farrell's distrust extended to all men. She would have liked to tell this persistent superintendent to go and hang himself, but reason told her that she must deal with these people, if she was to be done with the mess in which she had landed herself. Their questions still felt like an invasion of her privacy. She said reluctantly, 'He lost his temper when I asked him if there was anything in what you had said. Said I was all right for bedding, but I should stick to my trade. Then he told me I must drive him to meet someone.'

'Who?'

'He wouldn't say.'

'Where?'

'He never got round to that. I dug my heels in and said I wouldn't take him. That turned out to be a mistake.'

Her hand strayed unconsciously to the point where her side still throbbed. Lambert's eyes followed the movement, guessing what lay beneath the small fist and the navy fabric. 'What happened next?'

'He picked up my phone and rang somewhere. When they answered, he told them to get someone to the phone. One of the men you'd mentioned a few minutes earlier when you questioned him, I think.'

'Sturley?'

'That's it. He sent me out of the room while he spoke to him, but I cold see afterwards that he was worried. I'd changed into my dressing gown. He told me to get dressed. Said that I was going to be a useful bitch for once, instead of just an easy screw.' The pain of the phrases soaked her face in dismay, making her for a moment more desolate than all her physical hurts.

Lambert said, 'And you refused again?'

'Yes. I told him to get out. That's when he hit me. He was shouting obscenities at me, but I wouldn't cry out. I – I remember wondering how much the neighbours could hear! That's the way I was brought up, you see. Anyway, I think I must have passed out for a minute or two. When I came round, he was gone.'

Bert Hook leaned forward over his notebook. 'I'm sorry, but we shall need to check this out, if we can. Have you spoken to your neighbours since?'

'No. I wasn't anxious to show anyone my face.'

'I understand that. Do you think any of them heard what went on between the two of you in your cottage?'

'I doubt it. Mr Lambert knows that I live in the end cottage of four. There was certainly no one in the one next door to me at the time when this happened: I checked the lights. I was quite relieved about it at the time. Is it important?'

Hook said, 'It may be. An independent witness would establish that the argument and the assault took place at the time you say they did. With luck, he or she might even be able to confirm that Berridge left your place when you say he did, and alone.'

This time her face filled with alarm, not revulsion. 'You

mean that I might have gone with him. Might have killed him later that evening, at his place.' She spoke slowly, working it out for herself, her eyes widening in an accompanying horror at the realization of her position. 'God, why did I ever let a man like him into my bed?'

Lambert suspected that it was because even successful and self-sufficient women could be as lonely as anyone else. But that was not his concern. He said, 'No one is claiming that that is what happened. What Sergeant Hook is saying is merely that it would be useful if we could eliminate the possibility from this investigation. And you with it. That is why we shall be questioning your neighbours: it is very much in your interest that we should find someone to confirm the facts you have given us.'

They left her then, going out at her request through the back door of the premises. They were back in the Vauxhall, easing their way along the busy main street of the town, when the car phone bleeped insistently. The reception was not good between the high buildings, but the crackling made Rushton's message only more dramatic. 'We've processed the prints volunteered for elimination purposes now. And one of them matches with the print on the murder weapon.' Even through the interference, they caught the rise in his voice with the excitement.

Lambert was driving, so that it was Hook who said, 'Which one?'

'Ian Faraday's. Do we bring him in now?'

# 18

Gabrielle Berridge was unhappy in the midst of luxury. It was a bright spring morning, with the sun climbing and the clouds high. Through the broad picture windows of the penthouse, the views over the bright green Gloucestershire countryside to the top of May Hill were superb. Yet she could not wait to be out of the place.

Ian and she would set up house away from here. In the country, but in a different, harsher northern landscape. In an old stone farmhouse, perhaps. It must be different, to confirm the new life which was beginning for both of them. She tried to picture the setting for her new house, but it obstinately refused to define itself. The pictures which swam before her during the nights were agreeable fantasies, but she was impatient for the reality. She was looking out disconsolately when she saw the old Vauxhall turning carefully from the lane into the car park.

There was no sound from its engine through the double glazing, just as there was no sound from the birds which flew up at this disturbance of their concerns. She watched Superintendent Lambert lever himself a little stiffly from the driving seat. She told herself that he might be merely supervising the door-to-door enquiries which had brought excitement into the generally quiet and ordered life of the residents of Old Mead Park. That he might be here just to ascertain more details of the routine of the place from that cornucopia of local knowledge, George Lewis.

But, against her will, her mind pictured the tall man walking past the door of the porter's office, turning aside the slightly officious attentions of the rotund little man in his

145

green uniform, making determinedly for the lift. She did not think it odd when she heard a gentle tapping at her door: she found that she had already moved halfway across the flat when the summons came to open it.

The tall figure showed no surprise at finding the door opened so quickly. 'There are one or two things I need to tie up,' he said. 'I won't take up very much of your time.' He refused coffee, turned down even her offer of a seat. Nor did he trouble himself with the preliminaries of small talk. 'I'd like you to show me where your husband kept that pistol. We've established now that it was the weapon which killed him.'

She took him through the hall into her husband's study. She had not set foot in the room since his death. There might be too many ghosts. She made herself go without flinching to the desk and open the top right-hand drawer. 'This is where he normally kept the pistol. He was very careful, very methodical. Of course, he took it out with him, sometimes. I don't know when. I took care not to know what he was about in these last few years.'

To a policeman, it was a familiar disclaimer. Once a man was proclaimed a villain, those around him rushed to declare their ignorance about his activities. But it might be genuine, in this case. 'Did you see him with the pistol at any time in the week before his death?'

'No.' She spoke a little too quickly, almost before the question was completed, because she knew what he was going to ask. Her brain was racing ahead, wondering how much he knew. 'I imagine he was carrying it himself, or had it in the car with him, if that is what he was killed with.'

He looked at her for a moment, then nodded. 'Either that, or someone else removed it from this drawer. You didn't take it away yourself, Mrs Berridge, for any reason?' He could think of only one reason. And so could she.

'No. No, of course not. I rarely went in there. And he kept the drawer locked.' But a wife would have access to a key, in all probability, she thought. She braced herself for him to suggest just that.

Instead, he said, 'But when I tried the drawer just before

we discovered the body downstairs, it was unlocked, you see.'

She hoped her face was glassily blank, even as her mind reeled and she cursed her incompetence. She must have forgotten to relock the drawer after she had removed the pistol. 'I expect he took the gun out and forgot to lock the drawer.' How she wished that she had not said a moment earlier that Jim was careful and methodical!

Lambert said, 'Perhaps so.' He waited, as if she might dig herself into a deeper pit by attempting to extricate herself. But she had the sense to leave it, partly because she did not trust herself to speak calmly. Eventually he said, 'There is one other rather curious thing.'

She wondered what was coming now, noting that he had now categorized the business of the unlocked drawer as 'curious', and thus signalled that he found her explanation unconvincing. This felt like a job interview that was going all wrong: it was a long time since she had endured one of those. And the stake this time was her whole future. She said, 'I hope I might be of more help with this one,' and favoured him with a mirthless smile, trying to force humour into her dark eyes.

'Your husband had a BMW which was almost new, and an electronic gadget to open his garage door on his key ring. They were in the ignition socket of the car. Do you have a duplicate set?'

Gabrielle felt an immense relief, so overwhelming that at first she could scarcely frame an answer to the question. 'No. No, I don't recall ever seeing any.'

'But the car is almost new. There would certainly be a second set of keys. But we didn't find any duplicates, not in his clothes, nor in the car itself, nor in this apartment.'

She thought carefully, anxious to be of help on a matter that could only be innocent, as far as she was concerned. 'There must be another set, as you say. But I don't think I've ever seen them. Is it important?'

'Perhaps not. But anyone who had them would have had access to the garage and the car, you see. The fact that they're missing rather draws attention to that.'

She felt that he knew about the gun, was pointing up this as a suggestion that she was the one who had had motive, means and access. She longed to scream at him that she knew nothing about these damned keys. But that would only suggest that she did know something about the pistol. They were still standing, though they had moved from the study back to the lounge. She was thankful they had not gone into her bedroom; she felt that those cool grey eyes would surely have divined the place where she had hidden that pistol. She said, a little desperately, 'Was there anything else?'

'Nothing you can help me with here. We haven't managed to find anyone who saw you earlier on Tuesday evening at Stratford yet, but we are continuing our enquiries; we may turn up something, in due course.'

How unconvinced he sounded about that! Gabrielle wondered if they knew of her vain attempts to get Mr Allan at the River Crescent Hotel to tell them she had presented herself there before the theatre performance. Probably not: there seemed no reason why they should have been back to him.

Lambert thought carefully, then decided to give her a snippet from their findings. A sprat which might in due course bring in a juicy mackerel. He was almost at the door when he turned to her and said, 'By the way, we have now found a single print on your husband's Smith and Wesson pistol. I can't tell you whose it is, of course.'

Bert Hook enjoyed the drive to Stratford much more than Gabrielle Berridge had on the previous day. He had been up for three hours before he set out, working on his Open University assignment, stimulated by the television programme he had watched at 6.30. He had even found time to breakfast with the boys, a noisy interval of youthful boisterousness and paternal badinage. Bert had married late and happily: he congratulated himself anew on that.

As he set out on his journey, Detective Sergeant Hook felt the satisfaction of a man who already has a couple of hours of useful activity under his belt. The drive would be an interval of relaxation. And now that he was studying literature for his degree, Stratford seemed a place of pilgrimage, rather than just a bustling town on the northern fringe of their area. The hedges were flying green ribbons of hawthorn, but it was too soon yet to tell whether the oaks which grew so tall and stately in this central part of the kingdom would be out before the ash.

He came into Stratford over the same ancient bridge that had brought Gabrielle Berridge into the town on the previous day. But then their paths diverged with their concerns. Hook parked in the large public car park and crossed the lower end of the main street, eschewing the opportunity to be drawn into the preparations for the Shakespeare birthday celebrations to which the flags beckoned him. He moved a hundred yards to the Gower Memorial to the bard, grinning at the bucolic statue of Falstaff and the romantic one of Hamlet.

Bert looked across to the theatre, then strolled by the river for the short distance to its doors. The foyer was quiet at this time of the morning, but there were three people waiting for attention at the box office, and a group of pilgrims to the shrine were examining the still photographs from productions around the walls. He noted that the previous evening's performance had been of *Macbeth*.

It was ten o'clock. The rubbish bins in the foyer and on the terrace in front of the theatre had been emptied. But in the larger receptacles at the side of the theatre, Bert Hook found what he was looking for.

Ian Faraday was working in the rear garden of his house. That same rear garden which had looked so neglected when the CID paid him a visit. But he was not striving to improve that appearance.

It was true that he was getting rid of some of the winter rubbish. He had found the tinder-dry remnants of his autumn clear-up: the tops of perennials which he had cut to the ground after the season was over, prunings from shrubs which were getting too tall near his neighbour's fence, twigs and small branches from forest trees which had fallen on his lawns during the gales. When he looked round the garden, he was surprised how little he had done of late, how long it was since he had been out here. The new season's couch grass was coming up strongly among this detritus of the previous year.

But there was enough material for his purposes. He rolled up sheets of newspaper, built the dry sticks around them into the wigwam he remembered from boyhood, resisting the temptation to light his fire until he could see none of the paper, as he had done then. He was as impatient as a child to see a fierce blaze, but not for childish reasons.

The fire went well, as he had known it would. There was no need for the can of paraffin behind him. He piled thicker branches upon it, then produced a fine tall blaze with the dead conifer he had cut in two with his cross-saw. When the heat was great enough to make him stand back, he went swiftly to the garden shed, casting rapid glances at the bedroom windows of the two neighbouring houses which were the only ones to overlook his efforts. There was no sign of any observer.

He kept the clothing tightly bundled until he had it at the fire. Then he poured a little paraffin into the midst of the bundle, holding it tight again for a moment until the liquid soaked into its recesses. Then, after a final check that no curious eye was turned upon him, he unfolded the trousers and the sweater and cast them upon the blaze.

The paraffin made the column of flame leap like a live thing, twelve feet and more into the air. He put the shirt into the middle of the flames immediately, whilst the heat was at its fiercest. He did not want any trace of it to remain for anyone who came to rake over the ashes of this pyre. The clothes were soon gone, in that fierce heat. He piled more debris upon the fire, closing the chapter. It was, in its way, very satisfying.

He did not stay much longer with his fire. As the conflagration died down and he could get near the heart of it again, he raked the charred remnants of branches into the mound of whitening ash, turning the centre of the heap to check that no scorched vestiges of his garments remained for prying hands to recover, watching the subsidiary blazings with the gratification that comes from a task accomplished.

As his fire died, he was pleased to find no evidence that his sweater or shirt had even been part of it; not even a button had survived that Promethean heat. There was a blackened zip from the trousers. He took it and put it at the bottom of his rubbish bag. The refuse men would be round later in the day to remove it. Everything seemed to be working for him, today. With a last look at the gently rising column of smoke from the bottom of his garden, he went indoors to get changed.

He had showered and dressed, was almost ready for the road, when the phone bleeped in the hall. He hesitated for a moment, then answered it. It was the very voice he most wanted to hear: this must really be his day. As soon as Gabrielle had announced herself, he said eagerly, 'I've burnt the clothes I wore that night, as we agreed. No problems: they've disappeared without trace.'

She was scarcely listening to him. He caught the alarm in her voice as she said harshly, 'That man Lambert's been here. He asked about the gun.'

'But I told you, no one could know you removed it from Jim's desk. He didn't suggest you did?'

'No. Not quite. But they've found a print on that damned pistol.'

He said stupidly, his brain refusing to work, 'A print?'

'A single thumbprint. Ian, it can only be yours!'

# 19

The taxi-driver's name was Milton. It caused him fewer problems as his clientele became progressively less literate, but he still told them firmly that his first name was Billy, not John. Too many schoolmasters had enquired if he was the original 'mute inglorious' Milton; too many of them had said when his attention wandered, 'Milton thou shouldst be living at this hour'. Billy had inevitably been a little scarred; we are sensitive in our youth.

Billy Milton was twenty-nine. He had been driving his cab for three years now, after a series of other jobs had sailed on to the rocks of recession. He had taken pains to cultivate the air of experience that seemed part of the necessary equipment for anyone driving a cab. He was literally street-wise now, having an excellent working knowledge of the twisting thoroughfares of the ancient towns of Herefordshire and Gloucestershire, and even a degree of familiarity with the labyrinth of old and new that helped to make up the street map of the city of Bristol.

Nevertheless, he was feeling his way a little in this particular matter. Was discretion a part of the taxi-man's job? When he accepted customers, did he take on also an unwritten agreement to keep silent about things which might embarrass them? He had protected a few adulterers when questioned by their spouses, had even occasionally turned a blind eye to fornication four feet behind his head as he drove. Though that was against company policy, the tips had been handsome enough to encourage a little laxity. And Billy, while not vicious, was certainly no angel: that was the image he wished to cultivate. A Jack-the-lad who knew the score and had his own transport was much in demand with the girls.

But did you protect the clients whatever the circumstances? Even when the police might eventually be asking you why you had kept silent? Billy Milton found he was not as street-wise about these matters as he pretended to be in conversation. He decided he had better seek out a little advice. He thought about it for five minutes, whilst he ate his sandwiches in his cab and pretended to read his *Daily Mail*. Then he brightened: he had thought of someone he could consult without losing face.

George Lewis made Billy welcome in his porter's den at Old Mead Park. He shut the door, put on the kettle and unfastened the buttons of his green jacket, three actions which signified friendship on equal terms and even a degree of intimacy. They were companions in here against the uncertainties and injustices of the world outside.

George looked chubbier now that he had allowed his *embonpoint* free rein beneath his opened jacket, like an elderly woman who had divested herself of corsets. He gazed down with something near fondness at the young man he had seated in the room's only armchair. George was a man who had never been in a position to enjoy the luxury of giving patronage; now he felt very like a patron to this fresh-faced, vulnerable young man.

He had offered Milton an increasing amount of trade over the last year. It was automatic now that whenever anyone in the apartments asked about taxi services, he recommended young Billy. When visitors had to be picked up or the residents taken to the airport for their foreign holidays, it was Billy who was contacted. And he had been entirely reliable: punctual, cheerful and helpful with luggage when necessary. His efforts had brought profit to him and another small addition to George's standing as the factotum of Old Mead Park.

Now George smiled down encouragingly at his protégé. 'You said you had something to ask me,' he said.

'Oh, it's nothing really,' said Billy. It did indeed seem

153

unimportant, now that he had brought himself here. Perhaps it was something he should have sorted out for himself, after all. He did not want to lose face, even with friendly, unthreatening old George.

'Let's have it out and done with, then,' said Lewis, pouring the boiling water carefully into the china coffee mugs. He felt quite paternal: perhaps this is how it would have been, if he had ever had a son.

'Well, it's connected with that man who died here on Tuesday night,' said Milton.

'Was killed, you mean,' said George, pushing the bowl of brown sugar at his guest with the china mug of coffee. One had to give these lads standards; probably young Billy had chipped mugs and sugar from the packet in his bachelor flat. George opened the tin and put the ginger biscuits carefully upon a plate. His dead wife would have found a doily, but that would be a bit too much between two busy men of the world. He sat down on his stand chair. 'I wouldn't tell everyone this, Billy, but that Berridge who was killed was a right bastard. The police were after him for drug dealings, I think. *And* for murder. Don't you lose any sleep over Berridge – the world's better off without him.' His face hardened as he thought again of Charlie Pegg lying dead in the gutter, of poor Amy Pegg ravaged with tears when she shut the door of her house after his visit.

Billy thought irritably that he had never expressed any regret for the dead man; until this moment, he had not even thought about the matter. Perhaps George was just claiming a little part for himself in the dramatic events of that night: he had noticed from his fares how people tended to do that. 'I didn't know anything about this Berridge. He never used my cab. But if you say he was killed by someone on Tuesday night, that affects what I came to talk to you about.' He bit into a biscuit, munched it systematically. He was trying to come to terms with the notion that he might just have carried a murderer in the back of his cab.

George Lewis said comfortably, 'Whoever killed James Berridge has my sympathy. But I agree, it makes anything connected with his death more serious. What's worrying you, Billy?'

'I picked a fare up near here, on Tuesday night.'

'What time was that?'

'About ten o'clock, I think. Perhaps just before ten.'

The porter thought for a moment, going through his residents before he came back to the most obvious candidate. 'Was it Mrs Berridge?'

'No. I know her: she's used me quite a few times, dropping her off to meet someone.' He didn't mention a lover, wondering if Lewis knew anything about that. Lewis did. He knew even the name now, having chatted to the lady yesterday. But like his visitor, he didn't volunteer anything. For a moment, the two men sat sipping their tea, smug with a mutual discretion. Then Billy said, 'It was a blonde woman. She rang from the public phone down the road, near the pub. But she could easily have walked from here.'

'And what's your problem about it?'

'I heard the police appeal for witnesses on Wyvern Radio. I haven't said anything yet. But I wondered if I ought to tell them. It's just that I wouldn't like to get one of my customers into any sort of trouble.'

George smiled reassuringly at the anxious face of the younger man, pleased that the advice being sought from him should be so obvious. 'I don't think you have any choice, Billy. Superintendent Lambert has been here several times, and he assures me that this is a murder enquiry.' Name-dropping was another unaccustomed pleasure for George. 'I think you should tell the police all you can about your fare.'

Milton scrambled to his feet. It seemed clear to him now that he had no choice, but he was grateful to his mentor for making it so. 'I'm sure you're right, George. I'll get on to the CID at Oldford right away.'

'Ask for Superintendent Lambert. Tell him I told you to use his name,' said Lewis grandly. As the cab-driver reached the door, George's thirst for information asserted itself. 'A blonde woman, you said. The police will want the fullest description you can give them, of course.'

Billy stopped with his hand on the door handle. 'Yes. It was dark and I couldn't see very much.'

Lewis smiled, an old hand now in these matters. 'Nevertheless, you must tell the police about that fare, as soon as possible. You'll find they'll ask you questions about her which may help you to remember things.'

Billy Milton brightened a little: like the porter, he was not averse to a peripheral role in these happenings: it might even be good for business in the long run, if it gave him a tale to tell. 'I do remember one thing, though, now. She'd been knocked about a bit. One of her eyes was almost closed.'

DI Christopher Rushton was anxious to demonstrate how helpful his computer had been in the investigation. He was oversensitive about his chief in these matters: Lambert liked to protest his scepticism, but he was well aware of the time that could be saved in areas like record searches.

Rushton said a little desperately, 'Most of the search data is useful, but negative. For instance, there is nothing to indicate a gangland killing. None of our sources suggest a recent quarrel among themselves. On the contrary, business for Berridge and his partners in crime was going rather well. His drug deals were getting bigger, and the men he was buying from hardly appear in this country at all. There is always competition among the villains involved in London gambling and strip clubs, but Berridge seems to have kept his place in the pecking order and not been too greedy.'

Lambert said, 'Forensic have just forwarded their report on the package found beside Berridge on the front seat of the car. Drugs, as we thought. LSD tabs, in fact. To a street value of between four and five hundred thousand pounds.' There were a couple of token whistles from around the table, but no great surprise. Such sums were routine, nowadays. This package had been no bigger than the average briefcase. 'Presumably, that's what he went back to the flat to collect, after I'd seen him at Sarah Farrell's place. He must have known we'd have a search warrant within twenty-four hours.'

'Are there any hit men known to have been in our area

in the days before Berridge died?' asked 'Jack' Johnson, the sergeant who had organized the Scene-of-Crime team at Old Mead Park.

Rushton shook his head. 'None known to be active. There was a killing in Birmingham by one of them on the same night, so that rules him out. Of course, they're shadowy figures, paid killers. If they're not anonymous, they're not successful for long. There's always the possibility of one we haven't yet identified, but all the evidence is against it.'

Lambert said, 'And I can't see a professional leaving the LSD behind – not when it was worth as much as that.' There were nods from the others before he said, 'We know there are hundreds of people with good reason to wish Berridge dead. But there aren't too many who had access to him on Tuesday night. Let's go through those.'

'Right. The wife first, then.' The methodical approach, the ticking off of lists, was what Rushton liked best. And with reason: it was the basis of all CID work. Lambert thought he noticed a relish as the DI turned to the widow of James Berridge, and wondered again how deeply Rushton's desertion by his own wife had bitten. For the copper whose marriage had disintegrated, work could be either a welcome companion or a damaging obsession.

Rushton checked the read-out from his machinery. 'Gabrielle Berridge says she was in Stratford at the time of the murder. There appears to be a question mark about that.'

'Yes. She stayed the night there all right. Says she was at the theatre and produced a programme for *The Winter's Tale*, which was the performance that night. She could have picked the programme up at any time. They're prepared for the run of the play and not dated for particular nights. If this was fiction, there would be some variation in casting or some abnormality in the performance on the night which would trip her up in her account of it. We've checked with the theatre: it was a routine performance to a full house, with no hiccups that anyone in the audience could be expected to pick up.'

Rushton said, 'A full house? Doesn't that mean that they couldn't have booked on the night?'

'Unfortunately not. There are nearly always cancellations available at the box office of the Royal Shakespeare Theatre, if you queue for a few minutes before the performance. People have to book so far ahead to be sure of seats that it is inevitable there should be returns.'

Rushton said, 'There was an interesting snippet came in from the station at Stratford today. Apparently Gabrielle Berridge went back to the hotel where she stayed on Tuesday night yesterday. Tried to persuade the proprietor to say she had been there to book in before the theatre performance. No use, of course: he'd already been interviewed and told our man he hadn't seen them until eleven-thirty that night. He phoned the station to tell them about La Berridge's latest visit – I expect he has his licence to think about.'

'So she could have been at Old Mead Park at the time when her husband was killed. The porter didn't see her that night, but he couldn't say at what time she left the flats. Incidentally, I wouldn't put it past George Lewis to have turned a deaf ear to her departure if it was late in the evening. He was an old friend of Charlie Pegg, and he knows Berridge organized that death. I think he'd be quite happy to see his killer get away with it.'

Rushton said, 'Does that put him in the frame with the rest?'

'It must do, as far as opportunity and motive go. He had less to gain from this death than the others, but we all know revenge can drive men to do foolish things. What do you think, Bert?'

'Unlikely. He had the opportunity, perhaps more obviously than anyone. But you would have to say that about whoever held the job of porter in those flats. Just as domestic staff are always the first suspects in burglaries. They rarely turn out to be the culprits, if only because of that very fact. And George has been very helpful to the investigation: he's saved the door-to-door enquiry team a lot of time and confirmed many of the habits of the residents of Old Mead Park.'

'And he has no previous history of violence,' agreed Lambert. 'But we must remember that he had access and apparently a strong emotional drive: he's made no secret of his dislike of Berridge since he found out about Charlie Pegg.'

Rushton turned firmly to his own favourite for this crime. 'Ian Faraday. Motive obvious. Apart from the fact that he has been carrying on a serious affair with the wife of the deceased for at least a year, he makes no secret of his dislike for his employer.'

Lambert said gloomily, 'None of the suspects has troubled to disguise his or her feelings about Jim Berridge. One could wish for a little deceit in these matters: it sometimes makes things easier for us when we can get our teeth into a few lies.'

Rushton said, 'Faraday also says he was in Stratford at the time of the murder. But we have a thumbprint on the pistol from him. And Forensic say there is a rather smudged print on the other side of the handle which might just be that of his first finger. Hardly matters, does it, if they're so definite about the thumbprint?' Like all CID men, he tended to think in terms of cross-examination by a defence counsel.

Lambert looked at Hook. 'I think Bert has turned up something interesting about this Stratford alibi. It's an alibi, you see, for the two of them, if we accept that they were there as early as they claim to have been.'

Hook said, 'I went over there this morning. Had a look round the theatre. One of the things Ian Faraday produced was the stubs of theatre tickets for the performance on Tuesday night. The tickets have the date printed on them, you see, so that was much better evidence than Gabrielle Berridge's programme. Well, last night's play was *Macbeth*. And in the big rubbish containers at the side of the theatre – the ones into which the smaller bins from the theatre foyer and the terrace outside are emptied, I expect – I found these.' Rather apologetically, as if he saw the image of a triumphant conjuror and was trying to avoid it, he produced two ticket stubs for the previous evening's performance.

'So Faraday could have done just what you did. Collected the tickets by going down to the theatre on the morning after the performance.' Where once Rushton might have resented Hook's initiative, he was now delighted with it. It put Ian

159

Faraday right back where he wanted him: at the centre of this investigation.

'Quite easily. It was almost ten o'clock when I collected these. Faraday could have been down at the theatre before eight, if he had strolled out from the River Crescent Hotel before breakfast.'

Lambert said slowly, 'Both Gabrielle Berridge and Faraday have been at pains to establish that they were in Stratford early in the evening, though it now appears that they were probably not there. That implies that one of them at least had a pretty accurate idea of the time of death from the start. Before we even knew ourselves.'

'Which suggests in turn that Faraday committed this murder. And that his mistress either assisted him directly or tried to help him establish an alibi.' Rushton was excited as things fell into place. The instinct of the hunter must be strong if a man is to be an effective detective, and the scent of a kill excites all CID men.

It was Lambert who said with a grim little smile, 'But we have another candidate to consider. Especially in view of the information which has arrived in the last hour, I believe.'

Rushton looked round the expectant faces, human enough to savour this last moment when he held a titbit which had not been generally released. 'We have had a call from a taxi-driver, Billy Milton. He picked up a fare within six hundred yards of Old Mead Park at about ten o'clock on the night when James Berridge was killed. He doesn't know the name of his fare, but he has been able to give us a useful description. A blonde woman, probably in her thirties, with minor facial injuries. It sounds very like Berridge's latest mistress, Sarah Farrell.'

Lambert took up the story, filling in with information where speculation might have taken over. 'I interviewed Berridge himself in the presence of Sarah Farrell about four hours before he died. And I have seen her since the death. According to her, they had a major bust-up after I'd left them. Her story is that she saw him for the first time for what he was, and refused to cooperate with him. That may or may not be true. What is certain is that she was quite badly knocked about, either by Berridge or by someone else. If she was the woman picked up by this taxi, then the injuries probably occurred as she says they did. But what is interesting is that so far she has not admitted leaving her cottage on that night.'

'What was she doing near the scene of the murder on Tuesday night if she wasn't involved?' This was Johnson, speaking from an objective outsider's position; he had never seen Sarah Farrell.

Lambert said, 'I don't know. She rang for the taxi from the public phone near the pub, but she could easily have walked there from the flats. And she certainly concealed the fact that she had been anywhere near Old Mead Park when we interviewed her. And there is something else.'

At a nod from his chief, Rushton produced a small polythene bag. It contained something which glittered blue in the light, but it was so small that he had to define it for the men who stared at it. 'Sergeant Johnson found this when his Scene-of-Crime team went over the car. It's an earring. Found on the floor beneath the passenger's seat.' He looked back at Lambert.

The superintendent said slowly, almost reluctantly, 'We shall need to check, of course. But I'm almost sure this is one of the earrings I saw Sarah Farrell wearing at her cottage earlier in the evening.'

An hour after the unofficial conference of the James Berridge murder team had broken up, a woman came to the desk at Oldford police station.

She said she wanted to see the man in charge, then sat on the bench against the wall and prepared to wait. She was sixty-nine, but she looked rather older than that. She clutched her shopping bag to her chest beneath her hunched shoulders with both her arms, as if she feared that even here it might be snatched from her. She had pinched features; wisps of straight grey hair strayed untidily across the upper part of her face as she stared ahead of her and watched the station sergeant behind his barrier.

Much sooner than she expected, the constable came back

161

to her. She was ushered through doors which took her beyond the view of the public. The acned youth and the man who had brought in the lost dog were impressed in spite of themselves by the swift police response to this unimportant-looking figure. They had no experience of how a murder investigation speeds up even the most sluggish procedures.

The man in plain clothes stood up as the constable showed her in and gave her name. He seemed to her immensely tall, and quite young. But nowadays she found that most people seemed young, just as when she had been a girl almost all adults had seemed old. He was Superintendent Lambert, he said. She had an idea that was quite a high rank; it must surely be so, for he said next that he was in charge of this murder business. She felt a little shiver of excitement run through her at the very mention of the word: on a police-man's lips, it seemed suddenly more real. She sat on the very edge of the stand chair in front of his desk. She smiled frostily when he asked what he could do for her; men were always so polite when they thought you were going to offer them something.

'It's about the murder of this prominent local business-man.' She had read the local press carefully, as she did every week, and she produced the phrase with dutiful precision. 'I knew James Berridge.'

Lambert said, trying to hasten her on, 'So did several hundred other people, Miss Harding. But you know something special, perhaps.'

She leaned forward, her thin face like that of an alert bird, so that Lambert had the impression that if he made a sudden move she might peck him. 'He used to come to see that Farrell woman.'

'Miss Sarah Farrell? Is she a neighbour of yours?'

She was thrown out of her stride for a moment, thinking for some reason she could not pin down that they should have known these things already. 'I live next door but one to her. Not that I speak to her much. No better than she should be, that one.' She had still the traces of a Yorkshire accent, though she had lived in Gloucestershire for fifty years now. 'He used to come to see her, during the day, you see.'

She leaned even further forward, so that he was acutely aware of the straggly line of dark hairs on her upper lip. 'The bedroom curtains used to be shut, more often than not.'

Just as well, he thought, with eyes as curious as these around. 'It isn't against the law, you know, Miss Harding.'

'More's the pity.' His visitor sniffed, as if this deficient law was wholly the responsibility of the man on the other side of the desk. 'Anyway, I've come here to offer you my help, if you want it.'

'And in what way do you think you might be able to help us, Miss Harding?' Any policeman involved in the investigation of serious crime gets used to bizarre offerings from members of the public. Most of them are well meaning; some, of whom this woman appeared to be one, have empty lives which they seek to fill with a little excitement. The police have to listen, for the sake of the occasional gem of information which they extract from the dross.

Lambert had already decided that this woman had nothing of interest to offer. Long experience meant that he had a perception about people like Miss Harding. On this occasion, he was wrong.

She leaned back a little, then thrust her nose suddenly forward, like a bird attacking a worm. 'He came there on the afternoon of the day he died, you know.'

'As a matter of fact, we do know, Miss Harding.' He wondered if this eager spectator had noted his own visit to the cottage whilst Berridge was there with his mistress, and what she had made of that.

She looked a little deflated for a moment. Then she said, 'Well then, she's likely to be involved in his killing, isn't she? And your appeal said anyone who knew anything which might help should come forward. So I've come.' She sat back, triumphant in her logic, clutching her shopping bag even more tightly to her bosom now that the moment for her revelation was at hand.

Lambert was rapidly losing patience. He said, trying to maintain an even tone through his briskness, 'And just what is it you have seen that you think might help us?'

'I saw her, didn't I? In her garden, on the day after this

163

prominent local businessman was killed. Noticed that she was out there and thought it funny. 'Cos she's no gardener, you see. Has old Joe Philips in to do her little patch for her, she does, normally.' Miss Harding shook her head at such sloth and extravagance.

Lambert was interested despite himself. Any variation from the norm was of interest to a CID man; he had that at least in common with the thin column of bones and bitterness on the other side of his desk. But there was an edge of sarcasm to his voice as he said, 'And what did Miss Farrell do that might interest us on this rare venture into horticulture?'

She did not miss his scepticism. But she quite enjoyed it, coming as it did at this moment when she was about to surprise him. 'Tottering about on her high heels, she was, with her trowel in her hand.' She made it seem as if the woman had been naked, with her knickers in her hand.

Miss Harding giggled at the recollection of this unsuitable footwear. As she had not giggled properly for years, the sound issued from her narrow throat as a cackle. The noise surprised her, but she bent forward, right over the desk now, fixing the man who shrank from her glittering eye. 'She buried something, didn't she? In the back border. Right in front of her *daphne arbuscula* – though I doubt if that trollop knows the name of it.'

Now Lambert was interested. 'So she buried something. Presumably something small, if she only had a trowel. I don't suppose you managed to see what it was, Miss Harding?'

It was her moment. She could not have arranged it better if she had been allowed to script the exchange herself. She looked at him with a broad smile, her white dentures suddenly brilliant against the yellow skin. 'I didn't just see it, did I, Inspector?' She had forgotten his rank, but that must be right: they always used that on the telly. 'I noted the spot carefully for you. And today, when she'd gone to work, I went round the back of the cottages and dug it up with *my* trowel.'

'You shouldn't have done that, Miss Harding. You were trespassing. If we'd thought it necessary to retrieve –'

'I were safe enough. She's at work all day.' In her contempt for the interruption, her Yorkshire speech leapt out broadly at him across half a century. Then she thrust both hands into the recesses of the bag she had guarded so assiduously throughout their conversation. After a second, which might have been designed to heighten the effect, she held her right hand in the air between their faces. 'This is what she buried.'

She had at least had the sense not to wash away the soil from her treasure. A little Gloucestershire loam detached itself and fell on to Lambert's desk even as he focused on her find.

Swinging gently in front of his eyes with that gleeful witch's face only inches behind it was what he was quite sure was the missing set of keys for James Berridge's BMW.

# 20

George Lewis usually tried to get away from Old Mead Park on his day off. For one thing, people forgot that a porter was ever allowed time off, and if he was in his flat people seemed to assume that he was available to them. For another, he was aware that he needed to get away from the place if he was not to become dull and hidebound. 'Get out of that comfortable rut you wear for yourself,' his wife used to say, and George knew that she had been right, though he had never admitted it.

One of his problems was to find places to go. He was no great walker: not on his own, anyway, though he had explored the Forest of Dean pretty thoroughly in company in his younger days. And he had been to the cathedral and the docks in Gloucester too often for them to have any novelty left. Shops had never had much attraction for him, unless he actually wanted to buy something, and he had given up going to the cinema years ago.

But today he had no doubt where he was going. He had left his green uniform on its hanger and got out his new sports coat and trousers. He had had them five years, but they were still new to him. Certainly, they had not been much worn. He had thought at first that he would wear his best suit and his white shirt, but he had worn them for Charlie's funeral, and it did not seem right to appear in them today: better to pretend that that painful chapter had been closed.

He almost bought flowers. Then he thought again of the funeral and the wreaths and sprays. He bought instead a pot plant, a coleus whose bright amber leaves had fimbriated green fringes. He rang the bell, then stood back a little self-consciously from the doorstep with the pot in his hand. It was a long time since he had gone a-calling upon a lady; he could not remember how long.

But she had known he was coming, and there were not many seconds before the door opened. Amy Pegg had put on her cheerful, outside-world face to answer the door. She tried to force a smile of genuine welcome for George, but it would not free itself from the glassy smoothness of the rest of her face. Instead, she said, 'Come in, George,' and let him into the neat little lounge which she had shared for so long with Charlie.

Neither of them had much small talk. They sat erect as children who had been warned to behave well, feeling themselves strangers, united only by the memory of a dead man neither of them could mention. They realized in those minutes that strangers were exactly what they were; George had kept things up with Charlie, but they had usually met in the pub, happy over a game of darts, echoing long-gone NAAFI days in their easy male exchanges. Each had visited the other's house only once or twice a year, and when George's wife had been alive the two women had mostly talked to each other.

Now there were long silences between them, in which each was conscious of the other's desperate striving for a topic of conversation. Eventually, inevitably, they came back obliquely to the man who was their only real link. 'I thought the funeral went off very well,' said George.

'I think it was as he would have wanted it,' said Amy.

And suddenly, the awkwardness between them dropped away. Amy said it would not be easy, but she was determined not to be too dependent on her daughter, and George said that was the right attitude: he knew from his own experience. She said, 'You must miss Eileen,' and he admitted he did still, though it had become easier as the months and the years passed.

'Of course, I have my work. That keeps me busy.'

'Yes.' She wondered what she could find to keep *her* busy. There was not the same interest in keeping the house nice, now that there was no Charlie to appreciate her efforts. 'Do you have accommodation at those flats?' She could not remember the name of the place; she realized that she had not been there in the two years since he had taken up the job.

'Yes. I have a nice little flat. Well, not so little, really. It's designed for a married couple, you see. Nice to have a bit of space, when my daughter comes down from Cumbria with her nipper.' He did not say grandson. He was reminding her that he had a daughter, too, that he was not just an ageing man in search of company.

Amy did not want to discuss the details of his flat, any more than she wanted him to see beyond the lounge of the home she had shared with Charlie. She would have to offer to let him use the bathroom, she supposed, in due course. Well, he must have been there at some time before, when he had come here with Eileen. Somehow, it would seem more intimate, now that both their partners were gone. 'I'll make us some tea now,' she said, and shut the door behind her as she went into the kitchen.

She put the sandwiches she had made before he came on to plates, then buttered the fresh scones. When she had made the tea and put the cosy on the pot, she pushed the little tea wagon she had not used since Charlie's death into the lounge and shut the door carefully again upon her kitchen. Immersed in the rituals of this modest catering, she seemed to George a trim, courageous, wholly admirable figure.

The food eased the exchanges. It was a long time since George had had such daintily cut sandwiches, had tasted home baking. They reminisced a little about Charlie, each telling tales that were wholly to the little man's credit. George reminded her again of how his friend had saved his life all those years ago in Cyprus, and Amy said, 'He never talked about it, you know.' George had a second cup of tea, then began to wonder about how best to take his leave. He did not want to outstay his welcome, especially on this first visit.

It was at that moment that the phone, which was almost hidden behind the curtains on the wide windowsill, shrilled an interruption. Amy held it a little way from her ear and spoke into it cautiously, as if it were a live thing that might turn aggressive on her. George watched her affectionately; her diffidence with the instrument made him feel thoroughly a man of the world.

Then he saw the surprise in her face as she listened. She turned and held out the instrument towards him, as if he could reach his arm across the eight feet between them. 'It's for you. Someone wanting Mr Lewis.' She had somehow thought that everyone would call him George, as everyone had called her man Charlie.

He recognized Lambert's voice as soon as he held the phone against his ear. 'I gathered from the answerphone that you were off duty,' it said. 'I rang Mrs Pegg's house on spec. Glad I've caught you. Have you any idea when you'll be back? I'd like to see you.'

George said, 'Well, I shall be leaving very shortly, Mr Lambert. I should be home in an hour, at the outside.' He put the phone down, glad that the problem of how to get away had been solved for him. He said to Amy, 'That was Superintendent Lambert, the officer who got the men who killed Charlie. I'll have to go now, I'm afraid. He wants me back at Old Mead Park, to help him with the investigation that's going on there.'

George Lewis was quite pleased that the superintendent had rung him at Amy's. It showed her that he really had quite an important job. He was even a man the police relied on for information. He was halfway back to Old Mead Park before he realized that he had made no arrangement to see Amy again. Well, he could always ring. No sense in either of them rushing things along.

Gabrielle Berridge gazed out across the rising green acres of Gloucestershire and feared that she would soon begin to hate the view which had once seemed so appealing. Even today, with her lover beside her, the quiet countryside seemed menacing. It was no help to her that she knew the threat came from within herself, from her own awful imaginings, rather from the innocent hills towards which she gazed.

Even today, with her lover here with her, she could not rid herself of foreboding. Ian Faraday was sitting in the armchair which had once been Jim's, pretending to read his paper, watching her restlessness and feeling himself affected by it. Wanting to reassure her, he found all he could say was, 'I burned the clothes, as I told you. I've looked all through the house, and there's nothing anywhere now to connect me with him.'

'So you said. And I've looked through here in the same way. And there's no way they can prove that I removed that pistol.' She was irritable with him, impatient with his repetitions. This was not how lovers should be with each other, when the obstacle to their alliance had been removed. 'We've been through all this before.'

'I know. But they seemed to believe me when I gave them those theatre stubs. If they once accept that we were in Stratford for the play, they must rule us out of contention for his death.' He was going over old ground still, mentally ticking things off, trying to set his own mind at rest whilst ostensibly reassuring her.

Gabrielle said listlessly, 'Perhaps we can go away for a few days, after he's cremated.' She noticed that just as the police had become the faceless 'they', so neither of them today mentioned her husband by name. He had become for them a more baleful presence in death than he ever had been in life. When Ian looked at her, she said unnecessarily, 'It's been a big strain for both of us, all of this.'

They both knew what she was getting at; they had not been to bed together since Berridge's death. The event which should have liberated them seemed instead to have shackled a relationship which had once been so natural. She walked behind the chair, putting her hands on the neck she had caressed so often, feeling how tense the muscles were now. She eased his collar and began a gentle massage. 'Tell me again about what we're going to do,' she said. It was like a callow girl's demand of her first sweetheart, but he had once said he liked it when she behaved like that.

And he told her of the house they would have, hundreds of miles from the grave of James Berridge, after their quiet wedding in a little stone church. Of the new job he would have, perhaps now in their own company, where she could help him and be near him. This last idea was an addition to what he had said before the death, and he knew even as he voiced the thought that it was a mistake.

Their own business would be possible now. But it would be based on her wealth, from her husband's estate. It brought the man they were trying to ignore vividly back between them, even in the midst of their simple escapism. After a heavy silence, Ian said heavily, 'Anyway, whatever happens, we shall be together from now on.'

They remained like that, a Victorian morality painting that no one would ever see, with her standing behind him with her hands at his neck, and his right hand reaching up to hers, gently kneading her fingers, waiting for the answering response which the troubled woman could not give.

There is no knowing how long they might have remained thus if the phone had not rung on the table beside them. Their heads turned to it in unison. For a long moment, neither of them moved to answer it, as if they knew that the next step in the disintegration of their dreams was at hand. Then Gabrielle stepped briskly to the wall and picked up the receiver.

Lambert's voice, professional, not unfriendly, said, 'Good afternoon, Mrs Berridge. Is Mr Faraday with you, by any chance?'

Gabrielle kept her voice neutral. 'He is. Would you like to speak to him?'

'No, there's no need, I think. Not if he's going to be there for a little while. I'd like to see both of you together. In about an hour?'

She realized when he had rung off that she had not asked him what he wanted to talk about. But both she and Ian were in no doubt about the reason for this visit.

Sarah Farrell remembered during the afternoon that it was the day when her gardener tended the patch behind her cottage. She should have thought of it before. It was unlikely

171

that he would touch the back border, which was planted with shrubs. But at this time of the year the weeds were growing fast. He might just take the hoe to it . . .

The thought nagged at her, until anxiety became something like panic. Eventually, she said to her senior assistant in the travel shop, 'I have to go out for a little while. I shan't be long.' The woman raised her eyebrows: they were busy with the spring bookings, and the manager was not one to shirk the involvement. But Sarah gave them no further enlightenment.

By the time she had driven the five miles to the cottage, Sarah was in a state of feverish excitement. Old Joe Philips was not on the tiny patch at the front, though she saw that he had hoed out the weeds beneath the wallflowers in the narrow bed beneath the window. She drove round to her parking space at the back, then breathed a long sigh of relief, smiling wryly at her groundless fears. Joe had just mown the neat rectangle of lawn. He was coming from the garage with the edging shears. 'Home early today, Miss Farrell,' he said. The very sound of his broad Gloucestershire accent was an assurance to her that nothing was amiss.

'Not finished work yet, I'm afraid,' she said. 'Just passing through. You've got it looking pretty good. It's a credit to you.' She had suddenly realized that he might think she had come early to inspect his work, to check on his industry.

'No problem with that, m'dear,' said Joe. 'Not room 'ere to swing a cat round. But it looks right enough, I'll give you that.'

He looked appreciatively at the brightness of the Japanese azaleas at the front of the shrub border, and Sarah seized her cue from his glance. 'There's no need for you to touch that back border today, Joe. I'm going to give it a hoeing at the weekend. Time I did a bit for myself.'

Joe Philips did not think there was anything odd in this sudden urge to be involved. He had long given up any attempt to analyse the behaviour of the gentry, and working women were a new and exotic species to workers of his generation. Sarah Farrell was always friendly, and she often paid him in advance. That was good enough for him. He was

172

still looking at the border, and it reminded him of something. 'Cissie Harding was in here for a minute this morning. I expect she'd arranged it with you.'

For a moment she could not place the name. Then it came to her. 'Miss Harding from next door but one?'

'Yes. I can see through to some of your back garden from my bedroom window, you see. She seemed to dig out something from the soil, but I couldn't see properly. Perhaps she was just looking for that cat of hers – her's a devil for the birds, that one.'

Sarah looked at the patch where she had buried the keys: the soil looked freshly disturbed, but then it was only a couple of days since she had dug there herself. She had to resist the urge to rush to the spot now and burrow there before Joe Philips's astonished eyes. She said, 'She shouldn't have come in here without asking. I'll go and tell her so now.'

'No use now, I'm afraid, miss. She'll be round at her sister's this afternoon. Always is, on a Friday.' He hoped he had not got the old girl into trouble; she wasn't a bad old stick, when you got to know her. And they were the same generation; there was a sort of bond in that.

Sarah pulled her eyes from the spot where she had dug with her trowel, forcing herself to turn away when her senses were screaming at her to check whether her secret had been discovered. She drove back to the shop, her mind in even greater turmoil than on her journey to the cottage. She scarcely knew the woman. If the old biddy had found the keys, what did she plan to do with them? Sarah vowed that she would not be blackmailed, but she could not convince herself of her determination.

Though it was within half an hour of closing time, the shop was busier than ever, with the telephones shrilling their interruptions to the direct exchanges between customers and staff. Sarah vaguely recognized the large and comfortable figure with the weatherbeaten face who was standing outside the doorway of the shop. She thought at first he was a man in search of a family holiday. It was only when he introduced himself as Sergeant Hook that she was able to place him as the man who had unemotionally recorded her statements about her last hours with Jim Berridge.

He said, 'Good afternoon, Miss Farrell. Superintendent Lambert has a few more questions to ask you, I'm afraid.' Although he began almost apologetically, he knew he was going to allow no refusal.

But all she said was, 'Not here, please.' It was her professional self asserting itself: detectives seeking her out for a second time in a crowded shop would surely excite speculation among her staff.

Hook smiled. 'No, not here. We'd like you to come to Old Mead Park, please. There are some discrepancies among the different accounts of what happened there on Tuesday night, you see.'

He had watched her park her car. It was only two spaces away from his, so they walked together to the vehicles. With this large figure pacing at her side, Sarah Farrell felt already under arrest.

# 21

Sarah Farrell knew the way to Old Mead Park well enough. She was conscious of Hook and Lambert in the car behind her, escorting her watchfully. Perhaps if she had followed them she could have pretended she needed guidance, but she had a feeling they were now beyond such deceptions.

When she had locked her car and stood awkwardly beside it in the visitors' car park, Lambert came purposefully across to her. 'Thank you for your cooperation, Miss Farrell. There are some contradictions in the statements we have been given about this business. I thought it best that we got the parties concerned together; it seemed the quickest way to sort things out.' He turned without inviting any comment from her and went swiftly into the block of flats, leaving her to follow with Bert Hook. The superintendent seemed very sure of himself, she thought. That was rather disturbing.

George Lewis, observant as ever, had seen them arrive. He came out from his porter's office, buttons gleaming on the dark green of his uniform, hair immaculately parted and brushed over his sleek head. He smiled at Lambert, wondering about the woman who trailed twenty yards behind him with Hook, far too professionally polished to voice any enquiry about her. 'You said you'd like to see me, Super-intendent. I can see you're busy at present, but when you think I can be of any assistance, you know that I'll be entirely at —'

'As a matter of fact, you can help us now, George. I'd like you to lock up your office for a little while and come up to the penthouse flat with us.'

Even George's impersonation of Jeeves was not proof

against a little note of surprise in the voice as he said, 'Mrs Berridge's apartment? Yes, of course I'll come up, but –'

He did not complete the sentence, for Lambert had accepted his agreement with a nod and passed on towards the lift. As with Sarah Farrell a moment earlier, he had not even considered the possibility of refusal, and his energy carried them along in his wake. Bert Hook was left to shepherd them both into the lift. That was what sergeants were for, he thought without resentment. He had worked with Lambert long enough to feel the excitement of anticipation.

It was Ian Faraday who opened the door of the penthouse to them. He showed only a little surprise at the trio assembled behind Lambert. His own apprehension was such that he felt obscurely that there was some sort of safety in numbers. As the group moved into the drawing room, Gabrielle's only visible reaction was to add two more cups and saucers to the tray she had prepared in anticipation of Lambert and Hook.

Lambert looked at these preparations and said after a second's consideration, 'No refreshments just yet, if you don't mind, Mrs Berridge.' She looked full into his face for the first time, struck by a tiny nuance in his tone. She was the only person in the room who appreciated at that moment that Lambert, apparently so thoroughly in control of the situation, was himself under considerable strain.

It was Gabrielle who said, 'Shall we sit down, then?' and disposed them in a semi-circle around the ample easy chairs and sofas of the huge room. She realized too late that she had assumed the role of hostess, even in this macabre situation. The laughter which sprang unbidden to her lips at that thought would have issued as hysteria: she found her fist at her mouth to prevent it emerging.

Lambert said calmly, 'Thank you all for coming here. Sergeant Hook and I wanted to see you for a simple reason. All of you have told us lies.' He glanced briefly round the four faces. No one sought to contradict him, though Faraday glanced briefly at George Lewis, wondering what the porter's role was in clarifying all this, speculating about exactly how much he had seen. Lambert, finding his statement apparently accepted, said, 'Dishonesty is not an unusual phenomenon in murder investigations, unfortunately. The problem for us is to sort out which are the important lies: hence this meeting.'

Five yards from him, Sarah Farrell looked as if she was about to speak. She was exchanging looks with Gabrielle Berridge. Lambert, preoccupied with the solution to this murder, had almost forgotten that he had brought wife and mistress into the same room. But at this moment they looked more like companions in distress than bitter enemies.

He said, 'I take it we are agreed that there is no room here for false emotion. Every person in this room, including the two representatives of the law, is glad to see James Berridge removed from the world where he was perpetrating such evil.' He looked round the room, challenging them to contradict him, but there was no reaction, save for a single curt nod from the widow.

George Lewis, sitting on the edge of his chair in his carefully buttoned uniform, felt a need to account for the presence of a porter in this catalogue of hate for a murder victim. He said quietly, almost proudly, 'That includes even me. He killed my friend Charlie, you see.' Then when the others looked at him interrogatively, he added, 'Charlie Pegg, who did a lot of joinery work in here, and in the other flats. We went way back, you see, Charlie and me. And Mr Lambert thought I might be of use here.' With his credentials thus established, he settled a little more comfortably on his seat. He was the only person in the room on a stand chair; that seemed to him the appropriate thing.

Strangely, in view of these seating arrangements, the porter was the only one in the room who looked relaxed. Hook had produced his notebook and waited watchfully; Lambert was poised to conduct the interplay of this assorted sextet; the other three had given up any attempt to hide their tensions as they sensed a crisis.

Lambert said, 'Miss Farrell has left a hectic business to come here. Perhaps we should deal with her first.' Sarah Farrell's face showed that she thought that scarcely a privilege. 'Your statement told us that you quarrelled with the

177

deceased on the night he died. That he then struck you several times, then left you in a distressed condition at about seven o'clock on that evening, driving away in his own car.'

Inevitably, the eyes turned to look at what they could see of her injuries. The graze on her chin was scarcely visible now, but even beneath careful make-up the technicoloured flesh around her healing eye was apparent. She sat a little more upright in the armchair as she felt their scrutiny, then winced as the pain from the bruise in her side stabbed acutely into her poise. She had not consulted a doctor; she wondered again if she had a cracked rib. Her left eye had been practically closed when the CID men had last seen her. Now the swelling had declined and it was fully open, so that she was able to train both her bright blue eyes on Lambert.

She had made no move to confirm or amend her original story. Lambert spoke to the room at large, but his eyes never left the woman who had been the dead man's mistress as he said, 'One of the curious things about this case is that we never located the second set of keys for the victim's car. Until today, that is. This afternoon, a dutiful citizen brought them into the police station at Oldford.'

Sarah Farrell spoke like one in a dream. 'I had them. I buried them in my garden.' She felt rather than saw the surprise the statement brought to those around her.

'A foolish action. Why?'

'I – I panicked. I found them in my bag after . . .' Her voice faltered away as her eyes dropped to the rich green carpet.

'After you had driven James Berridge's car on the night when he died.'

Her blue eyes were too revealing. There was fear in them now as they flashed up to look into her tormentor's face. The others thought she might deny it. Instead, she said, so quietly that they strained to catch the words, 'How do you know that?'

It was Hook who looked up from his notebook to tell her. 'Your taxi-driver came forward and told us. It was no more than his duty.'

She nodded. A tress of fair hair dropped over her forehead and she was suddenly very weary. 'If it hadn't been him, I expect you would have found out from someone else.'

'I expect we should, yes. Especially after the forensic examination of the car produced one of the earrings I saw you wearing on that same night.' Lambert saw no harm in developing a notion of police omniscience among the rest of the group. 'You drove Berridge back here on Tuesday night, didn't you?'

'Yes. That was what we had the row about at my place, after you'd left us. I said I wasn't going to drive him anywhere, after what I'd heard.' She paused, staring past him now, seeing nothing of the room or the people in it, but only the horror of discovering the real nature of her lover in that small neat lounge of hers. 'I don't know how many times he hit me. Eventually I screamed that it was enough, that I would do it.'

'Why did he want you to drive him?'

'I never found out. I expect he had some idea that he would hide in the back of the car if necessary. And I'm sure he intended that he'd take my car to leave the area, when we'd finished here. He had things to collect from this flat, he said.'

'But you didn't stay to find out what.'

'No.' For a long moment, whilst all of them willed her to go on, she was silent. Perhaps she was only now contemplating the idea that she might have contributed to Berridge's death by her desertion. 'He checked that there were no lights on in the penthouse as we turned into the drive. Then he told me to drive right into the garage, because he didn't want the car to be seen. He left the door open and went up to the flat to get something – he didn't tell me what.'

'And what did you do?'

'As soon as he was gone, I slipped out of the car and was off down the drive. I took the car keys with me and slammed down the up-and-over door to delay him.'

Lambert said, 'You had your own set of keys to the BMW?'

'Yes. Jim had given them to me when he got the car, so that I could get into it if he was delayed when we met. On Tuesday night, he kept his own keys in his pocket and made me use my set. I knew he was going to take them back when

179

I'd finished driving – it was another way of telling me that we were finished.'

'I see. Go on, please.'

'Well, I found when I began to move that I was pretty well all in, and too knocked about to run. I thought he'd be coming after me in the car at any minute. I couldn't understand why that didn't happen – I thought it must have taken him longer than he'd expected to get what he wanted from the penthouse.'

She paused again for a moment, but no one else spoke. All of them were picturing the scene, with the injured, terrified woman on the unlighted country lane, stumbling through the darkness and listening fearfully for the sound of the engine of the BMW behind her.

Eventually, Bert Hook said, 'But when you got to the public phone, you didn't dial an emergency call for the police to protect you.'

She looked at him as if she had only just registered his presence, though he had come into the room alongside her. Perhaps his open countryman's face reassured her. Certainly, she seemed to dismiss the nightmare she had been reliving as she said calmly, 'No. I don't think it even occurred to me. Whatever Jim had done, I didn't think of betraying him like that. From what you now say about his activities, perhaps I should have done.'

She did not seem to consider the possibility that her story might not be accepted. Now that she had told it, she had a curious detachment, as if she was more concerned with getting the details right than with defending herself. Lambert looked at her for a long, intense moment, whilst the others waited for him to press her about the keys and why she had hidden them.

Instead, he said, his attention still apparently upon Sarah Farrell, 'Other people, who knew James Berridge for what he was, have also lied about that night. His wife, for example, who perhaps had most of all to gain by his death.'

Only Hook, who had watched his chief at work so often before, realized how subtly Lambert was playing upon surprise and apprehension to persuade people into speech. The fish rose unthinkingly now to the fly he had cast so precisely before her. When Gabrielle Berridge snapped, 'What on earth do you mean by that?' there was no outrage in her voice, as she might have wished, but only shock.

Lambert controlled his irritation that she should attempt denial, even now. He said deliberately, 'You were not in Stratford at the time you said you were on Tuesday night. Neither was Mr Faraday. I advise you not to try to continue that deception. It was unwise of you to attempt to persuade your hotelier to lie for you, Mrs Berridge.'

Gabrielle's face was very white now beneath the dark hair. Her mouth dropped open a little, then closed determinedly, as if she felt it had got her into trouble enough. It was Ian Faraday who said, more in puzzlement now than as an assertion, 'But the theatre – *The Winter's Tale*. Surely we provided you with enough evidence –?'

'The programme Mrs Berridge produced so conveniently was never very convincing. And Sergeant Hook discovered how you acquired the ticket stubs you thoughtfully provided for us.'

Faraday's head turned the few degrees to focus on the officer whom he had thought so placid and unthinking. Bert Hook said almost apologetically, 'I was able to retrieve the ticket stubs for the previous evening's performance as you did, from the refuse bins outside the theatre. They were still there at ten o'clock, much later in the morning than you discovered yours.'

Neither Faraday nor the woman whom he intended should be his wife made an effort to deny Hook's assertion. And the CID pincer movement continued to close in upon them.

Lambert said, as though stating a fact they would not trouble now to deny, 'You were here that night, both of you.' They looked at him sullenly, and he spoke briskly, like one impatient to have this over. 'It would be foolish to deny that, Mr Faraday, with your fingerprint upon the handle of the murder weapon. A bloody thumbprint, to be precise. It's my belief that you went away from the garage downstairs with blood upon your clothes. But no doubt you have disposed of them by now.'

181

It was so exactly the truth, and Lambert's tone made the actions seem so futile, that Ian Faraday's face was suffused with fear. It flooded in like a physical thing to replace the blood which drained from his cheeks. He struggled for a moment to say something, anything, which might seem like a defence of his actions. Instead, it was Gabrielle who forced out, 'Ian didn't shoot him. He only came here when I told him what had happened.'

Her voice was very low. She sat beside Ian Faraday on the settee with her hand on top of his. Lambert transferred his gaze from Faraday's face to hers, regarding her steadily, making no further attempt to rush things along, leaving time for the grave situation they were in to establish itself. He said, 'I advise you both to consider your position carefully. We have had nothing but a pack of lies from either of you so far. In view of the forensic evidence, particularly in relation to the murder weapon, you will need to give us a full and frank account of what you did that night, if you expect us to treat it seriously.'

It was a long speech for him, articulated slowly. It seemed to have the sobering effect it advised upon the couple to whom it was delivered. Gabrielle Berridge nodded twice in the course of it. When it was ended, she took a deep, shuddering breath and said in what was almost a monotone, 'I came home at about ten o'clock on Tuesday night. My husband was dead then. I found him.'

Lambert said dispassionately, 'Details, please.'

She looked at Hook, who was making notes in his round, surprisingly rapid hand, then continued in that curious, plodding tone, so unsuited to the dramatic nature of her material. 'I drove my car into its garage; it's next to my husband's. I was going to come up here and ring Ian: we were supposed to be meeting the next day, which he had taken off. Then something seemed wrong about the garage next to mine.'

'Can you remember just what that was? Was the light on in there?'

She wrinkled her brow in concentration, like a dutiful schoolgirl trying to provide an accurate answer. 'No. The place was in darkness. But I could smell something.'

There was a quick gasp from Sarah Farrell. Gabrielle looked at her, as if she had forgotten in her concentration that the other woman was there, and divined in an instant the reason for the horror on her light-skinned, damaged face. 'It wasn't blood, or flesh. It was a smell of smoke. A particular kind of smoke, which at first I didn't recognize. I realized later that it was what you get after a gunshot. But at the time I just thought that something might be wrong.'

It was a bizarre moment, with the wife trying to convince the mistress of her story, and everyone in the room picturing the grim scene which awaited her in the stark brick box where James Berridge had died. Lambert recalled her attention to himself. 'You didn't hear any shot?'

Again there was that strange, unguarded face, as she strove for accuracy. Shock takes many forms. Or this was acting of a high calibre. 'No. I'm certain I didn't. Just this peculiar smell.'

'Go on, please.'

'Well, I knew something was wrong, but I thought I wouldn't be able to get into the garage because my husband normally operated the door with his electronic gadget.' She seemed determined not to refer to Berridge by name. It gave her words even more the effect of a formal, prepared statement. 'But the door wasn't shut: it was pulled down, but not closed. So I slid it up and put on the light. There's a switch by the door.'

Lambert said, 'Just a moment, please. Miss Farrell, you're sure you shut the door when you left the garage?'

Sarah Farrell did not reply immediately. She could not see yet where this was going, but she was somehow aware that it was important. After a moment, she said quietly, 'Yes. I banged the door down hard. I was in a hurry, but I'm sure I heard the lock clang shut behind me.'

'But Mrs Berridge says that it wasn't quite shut when she arrived there.' He turned back to the widow. 'Carry on, please.' But Gabrielle had fallen silent, checking her story, trying to work out the significance of this for her. Lambert had to prompt her towards the horror they all knew was coming. 'And what did you find?'

For the first time since she had started this account, she sprang out of that monotone, with a flash of something near anger. 'You know what I found. My husband with most of his head shot away. He was lying on the floor of the garage, with just his legs in the car.'

'Did you touch him?'

'No. I think I nearly fainted. I remember leaning against the wall for a moment. Then I came up here.'

'In the lift?'

'Yes.'

Lambert turned to George Lewis. 'Did you hear any shot? Or see anything of Mrs Berridge's movements?'

The porter looked surprised by this sudden demand. 'No. I was in my own flat at that time. I didn't hear anything at all.' He looked at Gabrielle for a moment: perhaps in speculation, perhaps in apology that he could not confirm her account.

Lambert nodded, turning his attention back to the widow. 'And what did you do when you got into the flat?'

'I rang Ian. I could hardly speak. He calmed me down a little. When he realized what had happened, he told me to lock myself in and wait for him to come over.'

'And that is what you did?'

'Yes.' For the first time, she allowed herself a grim little smile. 'I put the phone down and just made it to the bathroom to be sick.'

Ian Faraday seemed to take that as the termination of her part of the story. He took over the account, and Lambert let him do so. 'I must have been here within twenty minutes. I checked that Gabrielle was OK, then went down to the garage in the basement. I suppose I thought she might have missed something, but the scene down there was exactly as she had described it.'

'Except that she has not described the murder weapon, or its position. No doubt you are going to tell us something about that.'

Faraday ran his right hand through his thick brown hair, as if it were an aid to concentration. He spoke carefully, as if each phrase was an explosive which would detonate in his

184

face if not handled with extreme care. 'I went into the garage, which was still open. Berridge was lying as Gabrielle described it, with his legs in the car, and his torso on the concrete outside it. I – I went to see if there was anything I could do for him. I don't know why: as Gabrielle said, it was pretty obvious that he was dead. But I felt for a pulse in his wrist. There wasn't one, of course.'

'Was the corpse warm?'

He looked as if there was a trap lurking in the question. 'Yes. Yes, I'm sure it was.'

'And the pistol?'

Faraday looked at the superintendent for a long moment. There was a desperation lacquering his features, as he wondered how he was to convince them of what he had to say now. 'I saw the barrel of it when I felt the pulse. It was just under his right arm as he lay on the floor of the garage. I lifted the arm and slid it out to look at it before I really thought about what I was doing. I scarcely touched it really: it was covered with blood.' He looked at Lambert to see if he was being believed, but found no comfort in that impassive, attentive face. He said lamely, 'It was a Smith and Wesson. I didn't move it more than a few inches.'

'Fortunately for you, the prints rather support your story. Anyone who'd gripped the pistol to shoot Berridge without gloves would in all probability have left more than a thumbprint and a smudged index-finger print. What else did you do at the scene of the crime?'

'Nothing. You were right: I did get blood on my sweater and trousers. There was blood and – and gore everywhere in there.' He moved his fingers to grip the hand which lay upon his on the settee, whether in apology or in search of comfort it was impossible to see. Every person's eye was drawn to the gesture, because there was so little movement in that large room. 'I came back up here to Gabrielle. She was almost hysterical for a few minutes – I suppose it was a delayed reaction to finding him killed like that.'

The woman beside him nodded confirmation at Lambert, as if she hoped to reinforce Faraday's credibility by the gesture. But it was Hook, looking up from the record he was compiling, who said sternly, 'Why the flight to Stratford? And why the lies?'

It was Gabrielle who answered him. 'I wanted to be somewhere, anywhere away from what was lying there in the basement. I suppose I knew then that I was going to be a suspect. The wife always is, isn't she? And I've wished him dead often enough in these last months.' Still she had not used her husband's name throughout their exchanges. 'And I wanted to be with Ian. We'd been to the theatre in Stratford, only a fortnight ago. Seen *The Winter's Tale* there, as a matter of fact. So it seemed natural to make that part of our alibi, when we found it was the play on Tuesday night. We booked our usual hotel on Ian's car phone, on our way to Stratford. We didn't get there until about half past eleven. But you seem to have worked that out for yourselves.'

There was almost a reluctant admiration in her voice on this last thought. Her delivery had lost its flatness and her voice was almost back to normal. Confession, however damning, brings with it a kind of catharsis, thought Lambert. He said quietly, 'Did you remove your husband's pistol from his desk, Mrs Berridge?'

Fear danced back into the features which had begun to relax. She could not control it, because she had thought the worst was over and had dropped her defences. She said in a voice suddenly hoarse, 'Yes. I had a key to the drawer, and I took the pistol away. But I didn't use it on him.' She looked wildly around her, aware of how unconvincing her denial sounded. None of the faces could give her any solace, though the hand beside her gripped hers even more tightly.

'Why did you take the pistol?'

'Not to kill him. I think I feared what he might do to me if he found out about Ian. And perhaps I thought I could threaten him with it, if I felt in any danger from him.' She was stumbling through this, and it sounded implausible, even to the speaker. She said despairingly, 'I just didn't like the idea of him having a gun in the place. I suppose I thought he might turn it upon me, if things came to a crisis.'

Lambert studied her for a moment. Whatever had been

her intentions when she had taken the pistol, they scarcely mattered now. 'And where did you put the pistol, after you had removed it from his desk?'

'In the top drawer of my dressing table. And before you ask me, I don't know how it got from there to the garage.' Her voice rose shrilly on the last claim, until it was almost a scream.

Lambert's voice was suddenly curt, as if to control this suggestion of hysteria. But his remarks were not directed now at Gabrielle Berridge. 'There are two people here who could have removed that pistol from where you hid it. One is Mr Faraday, but I don't believe he touched it.'

There was a long pause before anyone spoke. Then George Lewis said quietly, seemingly without emotion, 'I have a skeleton key to all the flats. Of course I have. Are you suggesting that I would have known where to look for that pistol?'

'Any burglar would, George. Your days of larceny are long behind you, but you're not stupid: you know what any policeman knows, that the back of a dressing-table drawer is the favourite hiding place for the innocent. When did you remove it?'

'It's the first time I've ever opened a drawer in this place.'

It was the easiest confession Lambert could remember. He was suddenly torn by a compassion for the criminal which was wholly inappropriate in a policeman. He must uphold the law, but in this case he had no sympathy for the victim and an understanding, even a sneaking approval, of his killer.

And now George Lewis was making it too easy for him. There was no need to throw in the forensic findings about the fibres on the rear seat of the car, the powder burns on the jacket in his flat. Lewis was not interested in deception; he seemed more concerned with the betrayal of his porter's trust than with the accusation of murder. He ran a hand down the stomach of his uniform, as if checking that in this crisis his buttons were fastened. 'I knew that bastard had a pistol somewhere in the place: he'd told me that when he first moved in. I thought it would be in the study. When it wasn't, I almost gave up; then I tried the dressing table on spec and found it.'

'When did you take the pistol?'

'Tuesday morning. After you'd told me about how Berridge had organized Charlie Pegg's murder.' He looked at Hook, writing furiously, then at Lambert. 'I said you'd need to get to the man who killed Charlie before I did, Mr Lambert. But I didn't murder Berridge, you know. I executed him.'

'Unfortunately, the law will not recognize that, as you are well aware.'

'Yes, I know that. But I thought until now that I might get away with it. I hoped it might go down as unsolved, if you thought one of his rival villains had gunned him down. I wouldn't have let any of these people take the rap for me, of course.'

He said it so calmly that they all believed him. Lambert said quite gently, 'You heard Miss Farrell say that she was quite certain that she shut the garage door when she left. But Mrs Berridge found it open. You were the only one who could override that electronic mechanism on the garage door, unless someone had used the second set of keys.'

Lewis nodded. 'The porter has to have that facility, you see, for security and safety reasons.' Again, he seemed more concerned to assert his function as custodian of Old Mead Park than to defend himself. He was even taking a grim pride in what he had done. 'Once I had the weapon, I only had to wait my opportunity. I knew the headlights of that big BMW, and I kept my curtains open. I thought I saw it coming in on Tuesday night. Then I heard the raised voices when I listened at the door of my flat. Once he had gone up to the penthouse, I came out.'

'And did you see Miss Farrell here?'

'Yes. At least, I realize now that it was her. I saw a woman go stumbling off down the drive, obviously trying to get away from him. I thought to myself, "I don't know who you are, my dear, but I'll make sure you don't need to run, if I get the chance." Well, I did get my chance, didn't I? I put on my gloves and got the Smith and Wesson. Then I crouched

188

in the back of the car and waited for him. I heard him swear when he found the lady was gone. Then he got out his own keys and threw something on the front passenger seat.'

'A consignment of drugs. That is what Berridge had come to pick up from the flat.' Lambert said it automatically, reminding them of the evil perpetrated by the victim, as his murderer reached the climax of his story.

Lewis scarcely heard him. 'I shot him as he got into the driver's seat. I put the pistol against his head and said, "This is for Charlie, you bastard!" so that he would know as he went. But maybe I shot him before I got that out.' He sounded as if that was his only regret. 'I had to get out quickly, because I heard Mrs Berridge's car coming into her garage next door. That's why I couldn't shut the door. I pulled it down, but I couldn't bang it shut and leave it locked because she would have heard the noise.' He turned to Gabrielle and said, 'I'm sorry you had to find him like that. I didn't mean to involve you.'

Lambert issued the formal words of arrest and Lewis nodded. He stood erect and smoothed down his uniform, ready an instant before the CID men for the procession into custody. They did not delay. Lambert said with a mirthless smile to the three who remained in the room as they left, 'Perhaps you can have that tea now.'

George Lewis was no danger to anyone else. He would plead guilty, of course. Hook speculated in the lift on how soon he might be out of prison, in view of his victim and the nature of his crime. Well, that wasn't their business, thank God.

They let him collect a few things to take with him from his flat. He was perfectly calm, showing no signs of regret for what he had done. When they had moved across the reception area to the doors of the luxury block, he took a last look back at his province, gave it a little nod of wordless approval, and moved off to the police car.

It was a still April evening, clear and calm. The sun had gone down. In the dark blue sky, the last of its light gave promise of a settled spell as they drove through the lanes. George Lewis savoured it for a while before he spoke the first words since his arrest. 'Tell Amy Pegg what's happened. She'll know I did it for Charlie. I expect she may want to visit me inside.'

They nodded, but did not comment. Perhaps the only thing left to him now was this delusion.